'What are you ...
Bren asked.

'And don't tell me ...
back off,' he con... ...
wouldn't have kissed me...' He lowered his
voice and dropped his gaze to her mouth.
'Correction. You *couldn't* have kissed me the
way you did the other night if you'd wanted
that. So fiery and real. Look, you're remembering it now, I can tell…'

She was. Her breathing wasn't quite steady.
Her blood heated, suffusing her face with
colour that she could feel.

'You kissed me because you wanted to,' he
said, his voice even lower, meant only for her.
'I know you, Nell, and you haven't changed
that much.'

Nell made a helpless sound in her throat. 'I—
I'm not looking to have this kind of
conversation in the middle of a hospital
corridor, Bren.'

'So we'll have it somewhere else. And don't
argue, Nell, because one of your nurses is
coming down the corridor and I suspect you'd
mind being overheard in a private
conversation a lot more than I would.'

Medical Romance™

is proud to present the final part in this
emotionally gripping duet by talented author

Lilian Darcy

Nell and Caroline work at
GLENFALLON HOSPITAL.

Glenfallon is a large rural community in the
beautiful wine-making region of
New South Wales, Australia

THE A&E CONSULTANT'S SECRET

BY
LILIAN DARCY

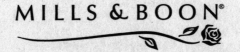

MILLS & BOON®

All the characters in this book have no existence outside the imagination of the author, and have no relation whatsoever to anyone bearing the same name or names. They are not even distantly inspired by any individual known or unknown to the author, and all the incidents are pure invention.

MILLS & BOON and MILLS & BOON with the Rose Device are registered trademarks of the publisher.

First published in Great Britain 2004
Harlequin Mills & Boon Limited,
Eton House, 18-24 Paradise Road, Richmond, Surrey TW9 1SR

© Lilian Darcy 2004

ISBN 0 263 83908 7

Set in Times Roman 10½ on 12¼ pt.
03-0704-44231

Printed and bound in Spain
by Litografia Rosés, S.A., Barcelona

CHAPTER ONE

QUIZ question.

Your best friend gives you the news that she's having a baby and, incidentally, getting married. Do you:

(a) say sincerely that you're thrilled for her?

(b) rush out of the room, sobbing?

(c) stay in the room, sobbing, and tell her everything that happened seventeen years ago?

Dr Nell Cassidy was extremely cynical about the value of women's magazine quizzes as a tool for self-knowledge and personal growth. This didn't stop her from subjecting herself to them, in secret, whenever they came her way, so she knew exactly how to word them and what they meant. Her attitude towards astrology columns was similarly conflicted.

Right now, she wasn't answering a magazine quiz or reading her stars, but was sitting opposite her friend Caroline Archer in the café at Glenfallon Hospital having a quick coffee, and she could easily have gone for any of the three options she'd mentally given herself.

She was (a) sincerely thrilled about Caroline's baby. She was also (b) painfully tempted to rush from the café in floods of tears. As for choice (c)…

Had it really been seventeen years?

Oh, she knew it was. Every line on her face measured the years, as did every memory and every career milestone.

And since she'd kept it all to herself for that long, why not keep it to herself forever?

'That's wonderful, Caroline!' she told her friend. 'I'm so happy for you, and for Declan!'

There. She'd successfully managed choice (a). If this had been a quiz, she could have awarded herself three points for it. Choice (c) would have earned her one point, and choice (b) would have given her nothing. Somehow, she always managed to score more points in theory than in practice.

'I'd wondered about the two of you recently,' she added.

'You had?' Caroline beamed. 'Oh, that's so lovely of you, Nell!'

'I hardly see why,' Nell drawled.

Narrowly avoiding an emotional catastrophe always brought out the sharp edge of her tongue.

'Don't you? Because it means you're a real friend.'

'Well, I certainly hope I'm that!'

'We tried to keep it a secret, and it hadn't been going on for very long. Only a real friend would have noticed.'

'All right,' she conceded. 'I suppose there's some validity to your analysis. When's the wedding?'

'Soon. Next month.' It was late August, and Caroline's baby was due at the beginning of April, she'd told Nell. 'So that I don't need a dress big enough to fit a bump.'

'Makes sense.'

Caroline smiled and patted her lower abdomen. 'One thing, though,' she went on. 'I'm concerned about how Kit's going to take this.' She dragged her teeth across her bottom lip and leaned forward. 'What do you think, Nell? How should I tell her? The way I told you, just as if it's a piece of simple good news? Or should I acknowledge that it must hurt her?'

It hurts *me*! Nell wanted to say. It hurts me terribly! Don't you know that?

If Caroline didn't, Nell knew it was her own fault...or her own triumph. She'd become an expert at concealing her feelings. The staff of the accident and emergency department at Glenfallon Hospital didn't believe she had any in the first place. Even those who knew better, like Caroline, or Bren Forsythe, had no idea which way those feelings ran.

Proof of this lay in what Caroline had just said. Her concern was all for their mutual friend Kit, whose life had been clouded by her infertility for some years now. A series of failed IVF treatments had broken up her previous relationship in Canberra. Now she was happily married to Glenfallon's obstetrician, Gian Di Luzio, and they'd adopted his little niece, Bonnie.

They'd also begun trying for a baby of their own. 'The natural way,' Kit had said a month or two ago. 'But we'll move on to *in vitro* if it doesn't happen soon.' So far it hadn't, and warm-hearted Caroline was concerned about flinging her own accidental but much-wanted pregnancy in Kit's and Gian's faces.

Which is as it should be, Nell decided. Kit's feelings are the ones to consider. I'm being selfish.

She removed from her mental tally the three points that she'd given herself a few minutes ago, then said slowly, 'How about telling her over the phone, Caro? You can acknowledge that you know it might be hard for her, but don't make a big deal about it. That way, if she's upset, she doesn't have to put on a brave public face. She can just put down the phone and hug Bonnie and Gian until she can get everything back in perspective.'

'That's a good idea,' Caroline said. She took a final bite of her Portuguese custard tart. 'That really makes sense. Thanks, Nell.'

'Any time. My hourly rate is very modest, too,' she drawled. 'Now, tell me—'

But Caroline didn't get to tell Nell anything more on this occasion. Nell heard the start of a paging announcement and then her own name. As usual, she welcomed it, rather than finding it an intrusion. For a long time now she couldn't have survived, emotionally, without her work.

A very experienced older nurse in the emergency department had the basic facts that Nell needed as soon as she walked through the door less than two minutes later.

'Highway accident,' Margaret Simmonds said. 'The driver is still trapped behind the wheel, and there's a road crew working on freeing him now. Extensive injuries, so they've already sent for the helicopter to take him to Sydney.'

'So who are we getting, Margaret?' Nell asked.

This department wasn't set up as a fully fledged trauma centre, but sometimes they got serious cases anyway. The principles of resuscitation and emergency treatment remained the same, whether at a large metropolitan hospital or a smaller regional centre, and Nell had built a good reputation for her department. This fact gave her a satisfaction she never even tried to put into words.

If the paramedics at the accident scene thought she

and her staff could handle this, then they probably could, she knew.

'Back-seat passenger,' Margaret answered. 'A seven-year-old boy. Unrestrained and flung forward after an impact at seventy kilometres per hour.'

'How far out of town?'

'Just a few kilometres. That sounds like the ambulance now.'

'Who do we have available?'

Margaret named the relevant staff, and finished, 'Bren Forsythe's just finished his morning list, too.'

Nell heard the surgeon's name with a familiar rush of awareness, but as usual she didn't let it show in her face. 'Can you tell him what's happening? Ask him to stick around? The boy could easily have internal injuries or fractures. I'd like Dr Forsythe here, if possible.'

There was no specialist orthopaedic surgeon in Glenfallon, but there were a few doctors, including Nell and Bren, who handled fractures on a regular basis and were comfortable with them. Despite a huge raft of complex personal history between them, Bren was the doctor Nell would choose to work with if she could.

As the ambulance siren grew louder, Nell's mind and body ran on two different tracks at the same time. She was used to that. She could prepare equipment and issue orders with one part of her brain, while at the same time mentally calculating a seven-year-old boy's likely weight—twenty-two kilograms, on average—and the size of tube she'd use if he needed intubation—5.5 and uncuffed, since he was under twelve.

How far would the ambulance officers have gone in their assessment and action? she wondered.

Not far, since they'd had a window of only a few kilometres of travel during which to work. For the same reason—the accident's proximity to the hospital—they wouldn't have waited to do much on the spot.

The boy arrived already strapped to a spinal board, with a cervical collar and oxygen mask in place. He had short, sandy hair and a face with freckles that stood out against his pallid skin. His eyes were closed and he looked limp.

He appeared around average size for the age Nell had been given, she noted, so the figures she'd already calculated should work for him. He was breathing but unresponsive, and they didn't have a name for him yet. Nell had a few names for the car's driver, probably the boy's father, who hadn't made sure his seat belt had been fastened.

Bren arrived as she began her initial assessment.

As usual, she recognised his approach purely by the rhythm of his walk along the corridor. He had a long, steady stride and his feet fell firmly but not heavily. She looked up just as he twitched the cubicle's curtain aside, and his familiar appearance confronted her. Sometimes it still seemed unbelievable that he'd come back into her life after so many years.

'What have you got?' he said. 'Could you use some help?'

'We can always use help,' she answered, looking away from him and back to their young unconscious patient before she spoke.

She didn't need to eyeball Bren Forsythe at close quarters to know what he looked like now.

He'd been thick-haired, loose-limbed and gangly at eighteen, with legs and arms he sometimes hadn't seemed to know what to do with. She'd thought he was gorgeous then. She'd loved his smell, which even in memory made her nostrils seem to fill with an oddly pleasing blend of soap and salt and eucalyptus. She'd loved the sound of his voice, with its fresh-minted deep notes. She'd ached for the feel of his body against hers.

Lord, so young! They'd both been so young! Now, seventeen years later, she *knew* he was gorgeous. He stood up to a comparison with any man she'd ever met.

At thirty-five, his tall body was packed solid with muscle that he kept well oiled and in shape with swimming and walking. He'd begun to lose his dark brown hair, but he'd taken an aggressive approach to the problem, as many men did now, and kept it shaved close. It always looked surprisingly soft, and had a dark gold sheen in the right light.

With his well-shaped head, tanned skin, warm dark eyes and darker brows, and the close-clipped shadow of beard on his jaw, he could have been a good-looking professional sportsman—the kind who was paid millions to promote tennis equipment or athletic shoes.

The faded green scrubs he still wore from the morning's surgery and the stethoscope swinging around his neck showed at first glance that he'd chosen a very different kind of career, however.

'Where are you up to?' he asked, moving to stand

near the monitoring equipment, which brought him into her field of vision again. His eyes flicked past her, then back to her face. If there was anything in their depths that suggested an awareness of the complicated past he shared with her, it didn't show.

'He's just come in and I'm taking a look,' she answered, then turned to the nurse who'd just re-entered. 'Margaret, can you get him on the monitor so we can check his oxygen level?'

This was measured by a simple finger clip and showed up as a percentage on a monitor. The monitor screen would also show blood pressure and heart rate when Margaret had had time to put the blood-pressure cuff on the boy's arm and heart leads on his chest.

'Eighty-one per cent,' Bren reported a few moments later, eyeing the green figures on the screen.

'OK. Thanks.' Nell didn't bother to comment that it wasn't a good figure. All three of them knew that.

'Let me check his airway,' Bren suggested, and Nell shifted a little to give him better access. She didn't like having him this close, didn't like sensing his movements just out of reach, or feeling the occasional warm brush of his arm, but her feelings didn't rate in this sort of situation.

While Bren checked the airway, she found minor bruising across the left side of the boy's chest and upper abdomen. His left femur and tibia were obviously broken, too. She could see that they were out of alignment, making his blue jeans look as if they'd been discarded untidily on the floor. The injured leg also displayed open wounds on the shin. Some bleeding, she noted, but it wasn't critical.

She wasn't even going to get his clothes off yet.

That could wait. She looked at the oxygen saturation figure again, and found that it had fallen, without the mask over his face.

'He's still unresponsive,' Bren said, working as he spoke. 'No facial injury. I'm getting clear sputum when I suction him, and no gagging. There's definitely a problem.'

'His oxygen's down to sixty per cent,' Margaret said.

That was an ugly figure.

'Can you get us a tube, Margaret?' Nell asked quickly. 'Size 5.5, uncuffed. I'll try a jaw thrust first.'

Working with deft speed, she made the delicate manoeuvre and it had the right effect. The boy's airway seemed to clear, but blocked again as soon as she released the pressure she'd applied.

'Oxygen by mask before you intubate?' Bren suggested.

'Yes, please.' It felt good to have a doctor here whom she trusted the way she trusted Bren.

With the mask back in place, they could get his oxygen levels up to ninety-three per cent, but no better, and ninety-three per cent wasn't good enough.

'OK, I'm going to intubate,' Nell decided aloud. 'Hold on here, little mate. Just let me do this, it'll be over in a minute.'

Guided by a laryngoscope, she obtained a good view of the vocal cords and passed the tube into the trachea. Listening through her stethoscope, she heard air entering the lungs on both sides.

'Oxygen up to ninety-five per cent,' Margaret said. She'd put on the blood-pressure cuff, her chunky finger working with surprising deftness, and Bren had attached the leads that would monitor their patient's heart rate.

'Great! You're doing great here, mate!' Nell told the boy, just in case he could hear. She spared a brief glance at his eyes, hoping for a flicker of his lids, holding her breath for it, but nothing came. 'Can you fix the tube in place, Margaret? And the cervical collar?'

'Heart rate is around 120, Nell,' Bren reported. 'Too fast. Pressure's OK—105 over 65.'

'What haven't we found yet?' Nell murmured.

Keep looking. Find out.

There was no deviation in the alignment of the trachea—the windpipe—and no further external signs of injury to the chest, apart from the minor bruising on the left side that she'd already noted. No indication of rib fractures when she palpated the chest. Tapping the area, she found its percussive sounds equal on both sides, but the stethoscope produced evidence of clear lungs on the right and coarse crackling sounds on the left.

'He has a pulmonary contusion,' she announced. 'No surprise there, I guess.' Bruising in the lungs would be hard to avoid after the impact on the boy's body. 'Possibly he's breathed in some stomach contents, too, but we can deal with that later. No fractures.'

'Leg?' Bren suggested.

'Yes. The leg. No kidding.'

She didn't hold back on the sarcasm. Everyone else in the department got used to it pretty fast. Bren would have to as well. He'd been at Glenfallon Hospital for three months now, and she discovered she needed the armour of her reputation more firmly in place on every new occasion that they encountered each other.

'I'm looking at the chest,' she finished.

'Stating the obvious,' Bren apologised. 'Sorry.'

'Let's get on with it.'

In an adult, she would have expected broken ribs, but a child's ribs were soft and pliable, and you could find significant internal injury even without fracturing. Nell glanced at the monitor again and saw that the heart rate had risen, while the blood pressure had dropped.

Internal bleeding.

The figures pointed to it, and the important thing was to find where it came from while keeping its effects at bay as best they could.

'Ventilator settings, Dr Cassidy?' Margaret asked.

'Try the respiratory rate at eighteen and the tidal volume at 220 mils. If the airway pressure looks too high, lower the volume.' She was referring to the amount of air going in and out, as she would have explained to her patient's parents, if they'd been here and wanted to know. Actually, in a situation like this, she wouldn't have let them anywhere near their son right now. Not till she had something better and more concrete to report. 'We want that pressure below twenty.'

'Heart's up to 130,' Bren said. 'Blood pressure at 98 over 56.'

'We have to get fluid into him. Margaret?'

'I'm getting there.'

'Four-forty mils, fast flow, warmed crystalloid, as soon as you can. Then get some blood so we can get him typed. Bren can you put a second line in the other arm? I'm taking a closer look here. His peripheral perfusion is poor, and he's cool.'

The boy's blood just wasn't reaching the extremities of his limbs the way it should.

'Capillary refill is slow,' she continued. 'Six seconds. The leg wound isn't bleeding, no other sign of external haemorrhage, no significant haemothorax, no abdominal distension. Give us some clues, little guy!' she begged the unconscious child.

Another nurse appeared at the edge of her vision, but Nell didn't take the time to look up. 'His name's Zach,' the nurse said. 'Zach Lloyd. Thought you'd want to know. They're still working to get the driver stabilised and freed. The police have contacted his mother and she's on her way in.'

'We'll have some good news for her by then, won't we, Zach?' Nell said. 'Hey? I bet you're good at school, aren't you? This is like homework, sweetheart. It's hard, but if you could smile for me? Open your eyes? Wouldn't you like to try that? Please, do that for me if you can.'

Working as she spoke, she stretched his closed lids open and checked each pupil. Equal in size, at around three millimetres, and reactive to light, but he hadn't tried to open his eyes on his own. Neither had he made any sounds before intubation, and he hadn't responded to her coaxing just now. She checked his response to pain and found that he extended on the left side and flexed on the right.

All of this added up to a score of five on the paediatric Glasgow coma score, and that was good. It suggested that whatever was keeping him unconscious, it wasn't serious and shouldn't last—provided they could work out what was making his blood pressure and heart rate misbehave so badly.

Professionally, she wanted Bren here. Personally, she was angry with herself for being so aware of him. It wasn't distracting her. It wouldn't. But she hated it all the same.

Margaret helped Nell to remove Zach's clothing and she reviewed his appearance, and his airway, breathing and circulation. No evidence of injuries that she'd missed. Good air intake on both sides of his lungs, but still that crackle on the left. The bag of fluid had already gone through.

Acting on the evidence that he had to be bleeding internally, although the site and the cause weren't yet clear, she decided on a rapid infusion of the universal type O blood, which anyone could safely be given. He needed more fluids, fast.

'I'm calling the radiologist for X-rays on the spot,' she announced. 'Ultrasound, too.'

'I'll phone,' Margaret said.

'Chest and pelvis?' Bren guessed.

'If there are no fractures, we'll try ultrasound, see if we can pick up the source of the problem that way.'

'Yep.'

'The heart rate's still rising. Oxygen level is falling. Blood pressure down to 76 over 45.'

'There's no evidence of spinal injury,' Bren said. 'Let's get him off the board, get those leg fractures splinted while we're waiting. Might be a while before we can get them properly set.'

'Call the anaesthetist?' Margaret asked.

'Yes,' Nell answered. 'I think we can assume he'll

go into surgery as soon as we have a better idea what we're looking for.'

'I'll help you get him off the board and call the theatre staff, get the place up and running,' Bren proposed.

Nell called Nurse Lisa McManus to help them remove the spinal board and splint the fractures while they waited for the radiologist to arrive with the portable X-ray and ultrasound machines.

As soon as he was no longer needed, Bren disappeared to summon the staff he wanted in surgery, and a few minutes later Nell got the X-rays she'd asked for. The results confirmed what she'd already detected, and ruled out a pelvic fracture, broken ribs and blood in the chest and lungs. The pulmonary contusion seemed minor.

'Whatever the problem is,' she announced, 'it's lower down.'

Radiologist Mike Kazias set up the ultrasound and they both saw the evidence of fluid flowing freely in the pelvic area and in the space between Zach's liver and kidneys. She phoned their report to Theatre One, where Bren and his team were already prepping for surgery, and a few minutes later Zach was whisked in.

His mother arrived, and Nell steeled herself to talk to her, knowing it wouldn't be pleasant. Kristin Lloyd was tearful, and her hand shook so much that the tea she'd been given threatened to spill. Nell almost took it from her, to save her staff from a slippery floor, but then Kristin took a big gulp and brought the level in the cup below danger point.

'They've only just got David clear of the car,' she

said, her voice thin and breathy. 'They're saying he's in a critical condition. What about Zach?'

'Zach's in surgery,' Nell told her simply, her own tone crisp and practical. 'I can't give you much news, Mrs Lloyd. Not yet. But I can tell you that a serious head injury or fracture is highly unlikely, from what we've found, and he's in very good hands with Dr Forsythe. I'll tell you more as soon as I hear.'

'This is like one of those television shows. They always say the surgeon's in good hands.' She meant the patient, but didn't notice her mistake, and Nell didn't correct her.

She felt helpless, and hated this part of her job, as always. She preferred the active phase she'd just been through with Zach. She functioned much better then, familiar with the fast yet controlled activity, the terse communication between herself, Bren and Margaret, the reassurance or the alarm bells given by those stats on the monitor.

She liked the detective work involved in ruling out one problem and diagnosing another, the delicate manoeuvre of intubation and the calculated risks involved in getting dosages right.

She'd never been confident about her people skills in moments of crisis and potential tragedy such as this one. She was terrified of empathising too much, and simply breaking down into useless, indulgent tears whenever she had to give bad news. No one needed that from her.

As a result, she often went too far the other way. She sounded too cool, too controlled, as if reporting on a car engine, not a living human being who was someone's son or brother or mother or wife.

'Dr Forsythe came to us from Melbourne a few months ago,' she went on, needing to give Mrs Lloyd more reason for hope, just needing to speak. 'He's operated in a lot of critical situations, and he's very experienced, up to date and competent.'

'Critical? Zach's critical, too?'

Nell's scalp tightened as she heard the way Mrs Lloyd had taken her reassurance. She'd picked up on that careless use of the word 'critical' and was now more distraught than ever.

Why don't I leave this task to some nice, motherly, grey-haired nurse like Margaret, who'd get it right every time? she thought, angry with herself.

'No,' she answered Zach's mother urgently, her voice still clipped and almost harsh. 'He's not critical. I didn't mean to give that impression. I'm sorry.'

'Oh. Thank goodness. I thought—'

'But I wanted you to know that Dr Forsythe could handle a far more serious, life-threatening injury than Zach has. I've known him for a long time, and I wouldn't tell you that if it wasn't true.'

'Oh. All right. That's…' Mrs Lloyd forgot to finish her sentence.

Nell waited for a moment, then said, 'Now, would you like to wait somewhere quiet until we have some more news? The kids' room is empty at the moment, or you could go to the café and get something to eat. You may not get a chance to later on, when you're with Zach.'

'I couldn't eat anything…'

'Try, Mrs Lloyd.'

Just get out of my department, so I can forget about

you for a while and catch up on everything else I need to get done.

People would have considered that a typically callous Dr Ice Queen line, if they'd heard her say it aloud, Nell knew. She hadn't meant it that way. It was simply a head-level recognition of the fact that Mrs Lloyd wasn't the only suffering human being she had to consider this afternoon.

'Will someone come and find me if there's any news?' Mrs Lloyd asked.

'Of course. Just tell one of the nurses where you're going.'

'I'm not going to stay away very long.'

Nell managed a token reply and abandoned Kristin Lloyd where she stood, in the middle of an empty corridor. She looked at her watch and found it was nearly four o'clock, then she went out and looked at the waiting area and the computer screen, and counted the patients.

Lisa McManus, on Triage, had just admitted a two-year-old with a high fever and vomiting, and there was a ten-year-old boy leaning against his mother's shoulder on one of the padded vinyl benches, nursing a sickeningly bent forearm and looking white around the lips.

Nell heard someone say the words 'severe chest pain' and didn't look at any more waiting patients. Mrs Lloyd wandered past, on jelly legs, in the direction of the hospital café, but Nell didn't acknowledge her, didn't want to get trapped in some exchange of formula phrases when there wasn't anything more she could give right now.

'Where's the chest pain?' she asked Lisa.

'Cubicle Three.'

She nodded. 'Right. Next I'll look at the two-year-old.'

CHAPTER TWO

BREN peeled off his gloves, mask, cap and shoe covers, stretched his shoulders, washed his hands in the doctors' change-room and went to find Nell to give her a report on Zach Lloyd.

It was after six o'clock, but he didn't think she'd have left yet. If there wasn't anything urgent to tackle in the department, she caught up on routine work, and if she was up to date on that, she manufactured busy little tasks for herself out of thin air.

Evidence that she had any kind of meaningful life outside the hospital was sparse.

This angered him, but he hadn't decided what to do about it yet. He'd only been at the hospital since May.

He still didn't know, in all honesty, how much Nell Cassidy had to do with his decision to return to Glenfallon after so long. For years, on and off, he'd thought about her, his emotions ranging from anger to understanding to remembered desire and back again.

Circling.

Like a shark, sleepless and on the hunt.

Nell had been a piece of unfinished emotional business in his life, like a splinter in his thumb. It hurt but the damn thing wouldn't come to the surface so he could get it out.

There'd been a significant period when he hadn't thought much about Nell, though—during his nine

23

year relationship with Liz. Then that had fallen apart, a year and a half ago. It still surprised him.

How come neither of them had seen it coming?

How could both of them have mistaken a deep and muddy emotional rut for actual happiness?

During his last few months with Liz, he'd started thinking vaguely that they should have children soon, if they were ever going to, because Liz had just turned thirty-two. He'd wondered why he didn't feel more enthusiastic about the idea. He'd felt responsible for Liz's happiness, and occasionally wondered if somehow he was letting her down. His hours at the hospital were heavier than he liked. She didn't complain, but maybe he needed to cut down...

A couple of times, he had tried to talk to her about this nagging sense that there should be more, but she'd been dismissive. They were good together. They understood each other. It was easy. Why go looking for trouble?

Then, out of the blue, Liz herself launched into a passionate affair with a colleague from work. She told him about it very quickly, remorseful but definite. She was moving out. She was in love. She was sorry that she'd broken their unstated rule about fidelity, but it had happened, and she could only be honest about it.

And the shocking thing was—he didn't really mind. He felt a guilty relief.

No, OK, he was hurt, too.

Hurt?

He thought back on the magic intensity of feeling that Liz hadn't been able to hide despite her best efforts, and remembered, no, hurt wasn't quite the word either. He'd felt a wistful envy. What was it like to feel that glittering, electrifying, unbrookable sense of happiness and certainty and rightness and belonging?

What was it like?

Hey, he knew, didn't he?

Wasn't that how he'd felt for two intense, emotional, utterly *right* months with Nell?

Ridiculous! He and Nell had been just eighteen. What did an eighteen-year-old know about how love felt, no matter how intense it had seemed at the time? Over and over, he'd dismissed the idea that he might have had it right, back then, with Nell, when they'd both been so young. And yet the nagging questions wouldn't go away.

His life in Melbourne had become unexpectedly awkward.

Comically so, at times.

He and Liz shared their friends, and even though there was no active taking of sides, it still wasn't easy. Liz and Simon moved in together, got married and conceived a baby, all within the space of a few months. People treated Bren with caution, and panicked visibly when he turned up at the same social events as the newlyweds, no matter how much he tried to show that he was fine with it.

He had evidence that couples would invite Liz and Simon to something, and only extend the invitation to Bren himself a little later, too effusively, if Liz and Simon turned it down.

'We really want to see you, Bren. Let us spoil you a bit. Are you sure you're looking after yourself, mate?'

Many of their friends had embarked on parenthood now. Liz and Simon, and Liz's growing pregnancy, just...*fitted* with everyone else better than Bren did—single, with the irregular hours of a surgeon at a big teaching hospital.

The herd instinct of his friends ticked him off, if he was honest, even though he understood the reasons for it, and laughed at it sometimes. He knew he wasn't the type to hang around like a fifth wheel. He had to take action. With the new gap in his personal life, he discovered that he was tired of his hospital-based job, and yet he didn't want to go into private practice and spend the rest of his life doing scheduled hernia and varicose vein surgery.

He wanted a challenge, and a change.

Go overseas? Switch specialties? Become a GP? Chuck medicine altogether and retire to the bush to keep bees or learn cabinet-making?

None of those options appealed, although the bee-keeping thing had a certain resonance, for some reason.

This was when he began to think about Glenfallon. He made enquiries. A well-qualified general surgeon with some orthopaedic and obstetric experience and a good track record at a large teaching hospital was always wanted in regional Australia. The board of Glenfallon Hospital would welcome his application.

Through mutual acquaintances in the profession, he'd made some far more discreet enquiries about Nell. He already knew she'd gone back to Glenfallon once she'd gained the qualifications and experience she wanted in Newcastle and Sydney. He didn't know where her personal life stood. His enquiries produced the information that she wasn't married, and no one seemed to have any knowledge about a serious involvement.

Nell Cassidy? Not much chance of something like that with her!

This was the impression that filtered through to him, via the friend-of-a-friend network. Now that he was here, in contact with her almost every day of the week, he understood why.

He found her at the nurses' station, on the phone to the hospital's small paediatric ward.

'I want to admit her,' she was saying. 'I don't like the fever, the listlessness or the throat. Tell us when you have a bed ready.' She listened for a moment. 'Yes, that's right.' Listened again. 'OK, thanks.'

Then she put down the phone and saw him standing there. Her gaze locked with his, she got a tight, panicky look in her eyes that intrigued him. She broke their eye contact too fast.

Three months ago, when he'd first seen her, he'd been shocked at how much she'd changed. It wasn't that she'd aged. She still had a great figure—womanly now, rather than coltish, curved in all the right places and none of the wrong ones. She moved with an efficiency and outward confidence that was surprisingly sexy.

Her hair was still that rich, burnished light red that he loved, like silk brocade threaded with gold. The pale skin on most of her face was still smooth, and her blue eyes were clear.

But the angles of her limbs seemed sharp, and her hair issued a warning: Watch out. I bite! The skin across her cheekbones and nose looked tight and dry, like a protective shell, and her eyes were so constantly narrowed—with stress? fatigue?—that lines had begun to form around them more deeply than in most women her age.

How often did she smile? he'd wondered that first day. Smile lines made a more pleasing pattern.

He could easily have taken a step closer to her right now and smoothed the tightness around her lovely eyes with his fingers, but he resisted the temptation, and hid it successfully.

'How is he?' she asked at once. 'How did it go? His mother's a mess.' She gave a short laugh. 'I've been avoiding her all afternoon.'

'You haven't spoken to her?'

'Of course I've spoken to her. But I'm not a hand holder, and after the initial interview there wasn't anything new to say. There will be, once you've filled me in.'

'He's in Recovery.' He saw her face soften fractionally as she nodded, and wondered if this was the extent of her care, or if she just refused to let herself show what she felt. 'He'll need further stabilisation and treatment, but he should recover fully, as long as the brain injury isn't severe. We're still waiting for the result on the CT scan.'

'I'm hopeful on that, based on what I saw,' Nell said.

'Yes, so am I. We found 700 mils of blood in the abdomen, so your aggressive fluid treatment was the right approach. He had a grade three spleen injury, and we removed the organ.'

'We'll need to talk to the mother about the implications there.'

'Pick our moment for that.'

'Of course. Soon, though. We don't want it to slip through the cracks.'

'We set the leg fractures. No problems there.'

'Any obvious cause for the spleen injury?'

'Lower rib pressure on the initial impact, I'd have to assume.'

'I'll tell the mother.'

'You're permitted a small victory dance first,' he told her.

'I don't do victory dances.' Her mouth tightened—or settled, rather, into a shape Bren could tell was habitual. Yep, there were those lines, putting fine, bluish grooves in her fair skin.

Suddenly, he'd had enough. Why did she let her beautiful, sensitive face react that way? Despite her striking form of beauty, she looked like a fairy-tale witch, sucking on a lemon, when he knew from experience that those lips could melt against the right man's mouth like red toffee in the sun.

'You should,' he said. 'Here, I'll join you.'

He didn't give her time to protest, just swooped down on her, closing the metre and a half of space between them in a fraction of a second. He slipped one hand around her waist and used the other to grab her tightly held fingers, then whirled her into a sketchy rock and roll jive that took them back and forth across the rectangle of space between the nurses' station and the corridor wall in loose, fast circles.

Her body felt warm and real, and the curve of her waist almost begged for a more thorough exploration, but she danced like a life-sized plywood cut-out, hissing furious protests at him the whole time.

Stubbornly, he refused to let her go.

An orderly came along the corridor to take the new admission up to Paediatrics, and he whistled and grinned when he saw them. Then he realised who it was that Bren held in his arms and his mouth dropped open in astonishment.

Nell's foot crunched down, forceful and deliberate, on Bren's toes and she twisted out of his grip.

'Matt,' she said to the orderly, her tone a cross between a bark and a sigh. If that was possible, Bren revised. He'd certainly never heard anything like it before. 'That was quick.' She tidied her hair, steadied her breathing. 'Good. She's in here. I'm going to look for Mrs Lloyd.'

Nursing his throbbing foot, Bren watched her go. Shoulders stiff, back straight, head high, walk brisk, not even tempted to look back at him apparently.

I could go home, he thought. I'm done for the moment. I'll come back later in the evening to check on Zach, but for the moment I'm free.

Wrong.

He wouldn't be free in any meaningful sense until he'd pushed Nell a heck of a lot harder than he'd pushed her just now, when he'd propelled her in that erratic jive step around the polished vinyl floor. He'd held back on this for three months, biding his time, wanting to learn who Nell Cassidy was after seventeen years.

But now he'd reached the point where he wouldn't learn anything further unless he pushed.

She had to oversee the hot, listless little girl's transfer up to the ward, and she had to find Zach's mother and give her a report on her son's surgery, so she might be a while. Bren went back to the change-room, peeled off his tired theatre gear and put on his street clothes.

Back in the emergency department, he made himself a cup of coffee and sat at the nurses' station, idly reading some of the terse, computer-printed notices pinned in various spots. Most of them, he guessed, had originated with Nell.

They began with phrases like 'All staff must…' and 'It is vital that…' and 'Under no circumstances will…' and he smiled and snorted and shook his head as he absorbed their meaning. He could almost hear her hospital-head-of-department voice uttering each one, with that tight mouth and those narrowed eyes.

No one would believe he could possibly want this woman, that he could possibly be interested in her, and be prepared to pursue her.

The thing was, they'd have been right.

He didn't want this Nell, the ice queen with the lemony mouth. He didn't want her even to exist. Where had she been, seventeen years ago? Had she been lurking inside the vibrant, passionate, intelligent girl he remembered? Had *he* done this to her, started her on this path? Had the potent end to their relationship made such a deep mark?

He intended to find out, although he didn't think for a moment that she'd make it easy for him.

'You're still here,' she said curtly, some minutes later, when she returned. Presumably she'd talked to Kristin Lloyd, although she didn't tell him how that had gone.

'Couldn't leave yet. We never finished our dance,' he told her.

'And we're not going to. I have more important things to do.'

'Later, then.'

'No. Not later. I want to see Zach for myself. He's probably gone upstairs by now.'

'Then I'll wait. Or come with you.'

'And by that time, I'll have to…' She let the sentence trail off.

'Yes?' he prompted her. 'You'll have to what, Nell? Colour code the paperclips?'

'Don't.' For the first time, emotion crept into her tone—a beseeching note that vibrated slightly, like a violin starting up after a melody-less introduction from the orchestra's percussion section.

'Don't what?'

'Do what you're doing.' The violin stopped, and she went back to the clipped voice and the tight mouth.

'What am I doing?' he asked, both stubborn and patient.

'I don't know. Getting in my way, for a start.'

'Let's go and look at Zach.' He did his own version of the busy doctor voice that Nell had evidently honed to perfection with years of practice.

Nell got even crisper. 'I can handle it.'

Bren matched her tone, crisp for crisp. 'I'm his surgeon.' He decided he could learn to enjoy teasing her like this, duelling with her, calling her bluff, beating her at her own game.

'Right. Of course,' she said. 'The mother was happy, by the way.'

'Really?' he murmured, deliberately quirking a brow. 'Happy that her son's going to be fine? That's a surprise. We don't usually get that reaction from a parent.'

Nell ignored his sarcasm.

'I've said she can see him now,' she went on. 'She's probably gone up already.'

'Have you eaten yet?'

'No,' she answered, apparently lulled by his surgeon voice. 'I'll get something later, on the way home.'

'Pizza. My place. You can leave your car at the hospital, and I'll run you back to it when I come in and see Zach again, later this evening.'

Her head whirled around, her mouth dropped open, her cheeks coloured and he felt a satisfaction building inside him like a slow-burning fire. So the old Nell was still there, somewhere, some of her, underneath the façade…

It gave him a place to start, at least.

CHAPTER THREE

'WHAT are you doing?' Nell asked Bren.

She was furious, flustered, breathless, disbelieving, but she managed to keep most of it from showing, and simply gave off her habitual icy annoyance.

'Making the sensible suggestion that we should grab a quick meal at my place,' he answered smoothly, 'since we're both going to be late, and we have things to discuss.'

'No, we don't.'

'*I* have things to discuss. But let's look at Zach first.'

'I don't see any need for us to have dinner together, Bren,' she persisted, far too aware of him striding along beside her.

He'd changed out of his surgery gear into a blue shirt with a subtly textured weave and a pair of dark pants that fitted his strong frame without being either too tight or too loose.

'But I think, given our history,' he said, 'you could do me the courtesy of agreeing to the idea, since it's important to me. It doesn't have to be tonight. We could make it Saturday. Do it properly. Dress up and go to Kingsford Mill. If you'd prefer.'

'No,' she answered quickly. She definitely didn't want to do that. Far better to get it over with quickly. Whatever 'it' was. And you couldn't eat at Kingsford Mill in under two hours. Two hours, just herself and

Bren, across a tiny table? No! 'Tonight is better,' she added.

Clang!

That was the sound of the trap closing around her. She'd seen clever mothers use the same strategy. Offer two choices with such confidence and authority that the child—or in this case the woman—didn't realise, until it was too late, that she'd actually wanted choice number three.

Nell debated a return to her original position—that she didn't want to have dinner with Bren at all—but abandoned the idea. That would look weak, or rude even, and rudeness and coldness were two different things. She'd made a safety net out of one for years, but tried to avoid the other.

She wondered what Bren could possibly want to say, after all this time. Was there any sense in rehashing it? Their adult selves had been formed, to a significant extent, by that long-ago summer. She had enough regrets already. If they talked about it, wouldn't she only end up with more?

As expected, Zach had been moved up to the intensive care unit now, after a successful graduation from the recovery unit. His mother was with him, still reacting with a numb kind of shock to the surrounding equipment that seemed to diminish his already small frame.

One of the hospital's most experienced ICU nurses, Kerry Smithers, was quietly checking his observations. He'd lost a lot of blood, and if his red blood cell count fell below ten on the scale they used, he'd need a transfusion. Bren had checked his liver during surgery, and it showed no sign of damage, but bleeding in the organ could develop later, and it was important to monitor blood pressure and heart rate for any signs of this.

'Mrs Lloyd,' Bren said at once.

He came forward, his body language conveying an openness and a willingness to connect which Nell knew she never quite managed. When she tried, she actually came across worse, so she'd stopped trying long ago. Happy to leave Bren to it, she listened to a murmured report from the nurse, given in response to her questioning look.

'Oh…' Kristin said vaguely, as Bren approached.

He saw that she didn't realise who he was, and explained, 'I'm Bren Forsythe. I operated on your son this afternoon. It went well, as you've been told, but do you have any more questions?'

'Oh… When will he be conscious, I guess, is the big thing? How long will he have to be here?'

'Well, the CT scan we did showed that the brain injury is minor, and he should regain consciousness within the next twenty-four hours. If he opens his eyes or speaks, let the nurse know, won't you?'

'Oh, yes! Oh, of course!'

'Plan on him being in the hospital for a week or more, although he'll be moved to another unit after a few days.'

Mrs Lloyd nodded. Bren asked her about family support, her husband's condition, whether she'd eaten and whether she was planning to spend the night at Zach's bedside. She answered his questions vaguely, but her answers made sense and revealed that she did have the right support.

'Is he going to make a full recovery?' she asked

finally. 'I mean, will he be able to walk right? Will there be a personality change?'

'Children have a wonderful ability to bounce back, Mrs Lloyd,' Bren said. 'I'm very confident, and I'm sure Dr Cassidy is, too.' He glanced across at Nell, and she nodded and smiled and murmured agreement.

She'd left the more personal exchange to Bren, since he seemed comfortable with it, and did it so well. He had a way of leaning down a little, to compensate for his height, and it made him look protective and concerned. His dark eyes managed to seem both alert and soft at the same time. You couldn't fake that kind of manner.

There was one practical, medical issue that Mrs Lloyd needed to hear about, however, and here Nell felt on safer ground.

'There's one thing you will have to be aware of, though,' she came in finally. 'Zach has had his spleen removed, as you know, and that will make him more prone to infection in the future. It's nothing drastic, just something to keep in mind. You'll want to make sure he has a pneumococcus vaccine and a flu shot each year. Zach's own doctor can advise you in that area, and we can answer any questions, too.'

'I can't think of any questions now. I—I'm sorry, I probably...'

Oh, lord, had she made Mrs Lloyd feel inadequate for not having sufficient questions?

'No, that's fine,' she assured Zach's mother. 'Of course you can't. It's too much to take in. Please, write things down when you do think of them. We hate it when we find out someone's confused or anxious about what's happening when we could have set their mind at rest.'

'Just as long as Zach lives. As long as he's OK.'

'I promise you, he's doing very well.'

She almost squeezed Kristin Lloyd's hands, but held back stiffly, as she always did, as if the woman's emotion was as contagious as a virulent disease. A couple of times, years ago, during her internship and residency, Nell had caught the disease and cried in the presence of a patient's family. She'd hated it. It was impossible to think or work properly under the influence of that kind of emotion. She hadn't let it happen in years.

Bren was watching her. She saw him from the corner of her eye, frowning in her direction and looking as if he wanted to say something to soften this awkward moment. In the end, however, he didn't, and they left the unit together a few minutes later.

'So, next stop, dinner,' he said to Nell in the corridor.

'Right.'

'Were you hoping I'd forget?'

'I thought it unlikely,' she answered carefully, and he laughed.

'You have the local pizza place on your speed dial,' Nell commented a few minutes later, in his car.

With his cellphone pressed to his ear, Bren grinned. 'So does every bachelor in Australia, probably. I like to fit the image. Yes, hi,' he said into the phone. 'Pickup, thanks. For Bren.'

He lounged in the driver's seat, half-twisted in her direction, and Nell searched for something to look at that wasn't him. He looked tired, but still relaxed and cheerful. Hadn't started the car yet. She forgot that she should be considering pizza toppings, until he said, 'Two large. One with mushroom and onion, the other with…?'

'Oh. Ham and pineapple.'

It was the first thing that came into her head. She didn't care what she ate tonight. Like most nights. Peanut butter on toast half the time, or a poached egg. Cereal with long-life milk from a box if she was really desperate and hadn't shopped—which happened too often. She should emulate Bren, and put the pizza place on her speed dial.

Sometimes Nell thought that unmarried male professionals had much better instincts about how to look after themselves than their female counterparts did. At other times, she decided it was just her.

Why, though? Why didn't she have the pizza place on her speed dial?

Bren repeated her order, ended the call and started the engine. 'I've got wine at home,' he said, as he turned out of the doctors' parking area. 'Or beer.'

'I don't want either, thanks.'

He shot her a glance. His eyes were so dark in the dim light of the car. Dark and dangerous. 'Scared, Nell?'

'Of drinking too much? No!'

'Of drinking at all. Of doing the tiniest thing to let down your guard.'

'What guard?'

He just laughed—again—and shook his head, and Nell wondered why on earth she'd lulled herself into thinking, over the past few months, that Bren's return to Glenfallon wouldn't be a problem.

Because he'd wanted her to be lulled. That was why.

The insight came suddenly, and she didn't trust it. His return had nothing to do with her, surely. When she'd first heard that he'd be joining the staff here, she'd had to work hard to handle it in the right way. She hadn't spoken of his arrival to her friends, and had been very careful to make her first mention of him to Caroline, in particular, in the course of a routine discussion about a patient.

Caroline had sounded startled to hear his name.

That Bren? she'd wanted to know. Bren Forsythe from years ago? Nell had continued to play it down, and Bren himself had behaved very smoothly. His casual, friendly conversations with her over work would have suggested to any outsider that they'd had a nodding acquaintance at school, and nothing more. She'd begun to believe that she might eventually be able to look at their past in the same way.

Now it seemed as if he'd had hidden intentions all along.

They drove in silence to the pizza restaurant, where Bren told her to wait in the car. He returned with the two white cardboard boxes, and she held them on her lap, feeling their heat blanket her thighs and smelling the aroma of yeast and tomato and salt and cheese.

She discovered that she was absolutely starving, with taste buds pricking and stomach like a cave. How long since she'd felt hunger in such a simple, intense form? She couldn't even remember, and didn't know why it should burn inside her this way tonight. Surely it was nothing to do with Bren.

'Here we are,' he said, turning into a small complex of semi-detached units, then into a short driveway. He pressed a button to open his automatic garage door. 'Just renting, at this stage, until I decide which ex-city dweller's unrealistic rural life-style fantasy I'm going to opt for.'

Unwillingly, Nell laughed. She always appreciated a slightly cynical twist in her humour, like a slice of lemon in a summer drink.

Bren came around to the passenger side while she was still unfastening her seat belt, and took the pizzas off her lap. She felt the curl of his fingers against her pre-warmed thighs, and the nudge of his shoulder into her arm, and couldn't help wondering if the contact was deliberate.

Impossible.

That would imply he was interested, and she wouldn't delude herself so far as to suspect him of that. If she'd noticed those two tiny moments of intimacy, it was only because she herself still felt—

No. Don't go there.

To distract herself, she asked, 'So what are the options? For the unrealistic rural lifestyle, I mean.'

'Well, a back shed with a potter's wheel and a wood-fired kiln, of course, so I can make ugly ceramics in garish colours that wobble as soon as you sit them on a flat surface.'

Nell laughed again, the sound fluttering up from her empty belly like a bird. 'Sounds good. You could give them as presents at Christmas to people you don't actually like.'

Bren laughed, too. 'That's a great idea. I'll remember that. Second option is an organic vegetable garden to promote bio-diversity amongst garden pests. I believe there are dozens of species of creepy-crawlies that love to eat broccoli, for example. But I'd have to say bee-keeping's the top choice at the moment.'

'Bee-keeping?' Nell echoed, startled at this one. Her father kept bees, out on the hundred-acre block of land towards Carrawirra National Park, where he'd moved after his and Mum's divorce. 'Are you serious?'

'No. Not remotely. I'm sure it's a lot harder and less romantic than it sounds.'

'Yes.' Although visiting Dad and helping him move his swarms or gather his harvest was one of her secret pleasures.

She loved the rich gold of the honey and the waxy slabs of honeycomb with their perfect hexagonal patterns. She loved standing out in the sunshine and fresh air, all kitted up in protective gear. Even more, she loved not being in charge, not being the one who had to know the answers and give the orders and get everything right.

She could appreciate the 'romance' of bee-keeping that Bren had alluded to, without the more prosaic side that went with it. Dad understood that it was a form of holiday for her, and indulged her in it. An only child, she'd always been her father's girl, spoiled by him whenever he dared. Mum hadn't been too tolerant of spoiling.

'No, seriously, I'll probably end up in town,' Bren said, opening the door that led into the two-bedroom unit. He had the pizzas balanced on one hand like a waiter. 'I like the older places. There's a street of

Federation-era houses I've got my eye on, and I've told the realtors that if any of those come up for sale, I'd be interested.'

'Well, if I decide to put mine on the market, I'll let you know,' Nell drawled. She'd found a printed leaflet from an agency in her mail-box a couple of weeks ago, telling her that there were genuine buyers looking to locate in her area, and that she might be surprised how much her house was worth in today's market. Did she owe the leaflet to Bren?

'You're in Grafton Street?' he said.

'Yes. And I'm not open to offers.'

Real-estate agents' offers, she meant.

Bren knew that perfectly well.

'I can be persistent, when I need to be,' he said, and he could have been talking about real estate offers himself, but Nell knew that he wasn't.

'Yes, I can see you need a bigger place,' she said, trying to sound matter-of-fact.

She walked around the small living-room while Bren went into the adjoining kitchen and got out plates, a bottle of red wine and stemmed glasses. Although the August night was chilly, there was a wall heater set on a timer. It must have clicked on a while ago as the room wasn't cold.

It seemed a little too crowded, however. The furnishings had been bought for a bigger place. There was a large television set and a sound system, each fitting in its own customised cabinet. Bren had a three-seater couch and two matching armchairs as well, a guitar in a black vinyl case stuck behind the couch and a whole wall of shelves stacked two layers deep with books that only seemed grudgingly to make room for the exotic ornaments also arranged there.

'You have some interesting things. Nice things,' she said, struggling.

This was so personal, two tired people alone at night, about to share a meal that you couldn't possibly eat with knives and forks.

'Yes, I did pretty well out of the divorce,' Bren answered.

'You're divorced? But I thought you were never...'

She stopped, and heard a dull *thlop* as the wine cork pulled free, before he replied easily, 'You're right. There was no divorce.'

He looked up at her for a moment, his dark eyes narrowed in a half-smile, but his lips still straight and steady. Nell remembered that he'd always smiled more with his eyes than with his mouth. It made his smiles seem as if the two of them were sharing a sweet secret.

She'd rarely encountered eyes with such depth and warmth. With his uncompromising haircut and well-built body, the contrasting impressions of strength and kindness that he gave off drew her in, tempting her to let down her guard.

'Technically,' he went on, 'since Liz and I were never married, we didn't need a divorce. Convenient. But we'd been together for nine years, and in that length of time the ownership of personal possessions can get just as tangled and hard to track, with a marriage certificate or without one.'

'I suppose so,' she agreed, wondering what had happened in their relationship to end it after such a long time.

'What else do you want to know about Liz and me?' he said.

Had he read her mind?

'Nothing,' she answered quickly. 'I wouldn't dream of—'

'Go on,' he prompted, still watching her with those incredible eyes. He had the opened wine bottle in his hand, tilted a little and hovering over the glasses, but he didn't pour. The half-completed action seemed to slow the passage of time in the room. 'Let's catch up a bit, fill each other in. I don't mind talking about it. In fact, I'd like to.'

'No!' She sensed another trap, deliberately laid.

He shrugged, filled their glasses at last, carried them to the small round table and opened the pizza boxes. The aroma strengthened at once, and Nell's mouth almost ached with impatience to take her first bite. She sat down and took one of the hot wedges in her hand, opened her mouth and instinctively closed her eyes.

Oh, it was good...

She opened them some seconds later, ready for her second mouthful of salt and heat and yeast, sweetness and stretchy cheese, and found Bren's eyes fixed on her face again. This time he was grinning. 'I like a woman who appreciates her food,' he said.

She flushed, felt her pulses quicken, and was furious with herself. 'I...uh, yes, I'm pretty hungry,' she admitted, and grabbed her wine.

'You wanted to know about Liz and me,' he said, his dark eyes daring her to challenge the brazen untruth.

'You obviously want to tell me,' she retorted.

'I think it would be good to get some of my baggage

on the table. I'd like some of yours, too. How are your parents? Still in Glenfallon?'

'Dad is. Mum's in Brisbane now. They divorced about fifteen years ago, and she moved north and got the accounting degree she'd always wanted. She has her own business, and is doing very well. She's still a relatively young woman, at fifty-four.'

'Are you closer to her now?'

'No, not really.'

'Would you like to be?'

I'm afraid to be.

Afraid of what she'd say, what she'd feel.

'Didn't I want to hear about you and Liz?' she said aloud.

'That's right. Let's not get distracted. She fell in love,' Bren said simply. 'It was…odd, really. We both casually assumed that we did love each other, in the way we were supposed to, until she got struck by a thunderbolt one day, which made us realise that we'd only been calling it love when, in fact, it was a whole lot of other things.'

'What things?'

'Safety, convenience, narrow horizons, for both of us. That's why I can't be angry with her, even though I hope in her position I'd have had the courage to end one relationship before starting on the next. It got me thinking.'

'Yes?'

'About you and me.'

I walked into that, didn't I?

'That was a long time ago, Bren. Over so quickly.'

Undone, almost, as if it had never happened at all.

'It shaped us.'

'You were very angry with me,' she reminded him.

'At the time, yes.'

'So angry that I'm surprised...' She waved her hands, still holding wineglass and pizza.

He looked startled. 'Surprised about what?'

'That you're here, talking to me. That you're in Glenfallon at all. That you don't seem to be angry any more.'

'Angry after seventeen years?'

'I let you down—abandoned you—pretty badly.'

She'd whipped herself over it ever since, hated herself for it, and had never really forgiven her mother for the influence she'd exerted. More, she'd never forgiven herself for succumbing to it. She should have had more faith and more courage, in a lot of areas. Bren might not feel angry after seventeen years, but she still felt racked.

Bren had had cancer—a papillary carcinoma of the thyroid that was rare in young men, more common in young women. He'd come to her with the devastating news in early January, when she'd already been in a state of complete turmoil. Their relationship had erupted into being just two months earlier, with an intensity she'd found overwhelming—wonderful and frightening at the same time.

Thinking back, she could almost feel it again. They'd all been waiting on tenterhooks for exam results to come out. Would she do well enough to get into medicine, as she wanted? Her mother had put on a lot of pressure over the years.

'You must take your future seriously,' Mum had said, so many times. 'You have the ability. It would be criminal not to use it, to get deflected.'

Nell was placed under strict curfews all year so she could study, and she could well imagine, even now, the tirade she'd have received from her mother if she'd fallen short of the required score.

When exams were over, the curfews were lifted, the immediate pressure was off and they all went a little crazy. For the first time, Mum turned a blind eye to the late hours she kept. She and Bren spent every spare moment together, talking, driving, swimming naked in the river after dark.

They lost their virginity together.

Awkwardly.

Full of trust and forgiveness and promises.

Solemnly, they taught each other, and soon there was no more awkwardness and it was wonderful. They grew careless. Naïvely, Nell didn't think it would matter. She'd just begun to suspect that it might have mattered after all when Bren received his shocking diagnosis. The outlook for his future was good, after treatment, but by no means assured. It wouldn't be an easy road.

He begged her to marry him straight away. Grasping at straws, she eventually understood, grasping at life itself.

His family were moving to Melbourne, he told her, and he would have his treatment there. He would defer his studies for a year until his prognosis was clearer, but he didn't want to defer their marriage. If the treatment failed, he wanted Nell with him all the way. Financially, they'd manage. He didn't know how, but they would.

She was distraught, a mess. His emotion frightened her, and his demands for an instant agreement from her made it even harder. She insisted that she needed time to think about what was possible. She had still been in major denial about the inkling of another life-altering event in her future. Then, in her state of turmoil, she did the worst possible thing. She told her mother.

'You panicked,' Bren said simply, and he was right. 'Since I panicked, too, and tried to cling to you like a drowning animal, yes, I was furious and hurt and I did feel abandoned. But we were only eighteen. I asked far too much of you. I'm not surprised you couldn't give it. It would have been a disaster if you had.'

Nell spoke through a tight throat. 'Really?'

'Yes!' He swore. 'You don't honestly think I blame you, do you? Still? After all the years I've had to gain some perspective? After all the outlandish emotions I've seen in people since, in a medical context and out of it?'

'I blame myself,' she said. 'I shouldn't have just turned tail and run. I should never have hidden behind my mother's skirts like a child.'

'I got the impression your mother was very happy that you did.'

'I should have stood up to her.'

'How would you feel, now, if you had an eighteen-year-old daughter, and she was proposing to marry a kid her own age, with no job and no money, whom she'd been involved with for just a couple of months, and who might be terminally ill?'

Nell gave a shaky laugh. 'If I had an eighteen-year-old daughter…? Lord, it's almost possible, isn't it?' Her throat tightened further, and her voice came out scratchy and harsh. 'Sixteen. Sixteen is possible.'

With a birthday this month.

'What would you tell her?' Bren said.

'Not what my mother told me. I hope. Maybe I would. I'm getting more and more like her, I often think. But, no, I hope I wouldn't tell my daughter to turn her back and cut off. Not completely. We didn't have to get married, you and I. I could have stayed involved, stayed a part of your life.'

'Do you think so?' he asked slowly. She watched the way his mouth moved, mesmerised by it. 'Don't you think that maybe it was all or nothing for us back then?'

'Are you trying to convince me to forgive myself?'

'Dear God, you should! You should have forgiven yourself long ago!'

'Hmm.' She didn't trust herself to speak, and felt shaken by this evidence of the way he'd matured, the thought he must have put in. She knew she'd tackled the past differently.

Instead of answering, she stared down at her wine-glass and her plate, waiting for Bren to torment her still further, holding her old, familiar guilt and pain like a hot rock cradled against her stomach.

Would she ever tell him about the other part of it that she couldn't forgive herself for? Would she ever tell him about the baby?

For seventeen years she hadn't, and surely now there wasn't anything to say. The baby hadn't been a factor to consider for very long. When she and Bren had split up, she'd still been attributing her lateness to a cycle that had been wildly irregular at the time. A week later, when Bren had already gone to Melbourne, Nell's mother had asked some searching questions, forbidden her to tell a soul and bought the testing kit for her.

Positive.

But the baby had only existed, even as an abstract promise, for a couple of weeks, too tiny for her even to have known its gender. Why did Bren need to hear about it after all this time?

He had evidently decided they'd talked enough about personal things, in any case. 'Feel like some music?' he asked.

'That would be nice.'

'I have an eclectic collection. What do you fancy?'

'Um, I don't know. Something eclectic?' She was teasing him—with a huge degree of effort, admittedly—for using a word like that, and he knew it.

A glint appeared in those magical eyes. 'OK. You asked for it.'

He went to his CD rack, pulled something out and put it on, while Nell felt the remainder of her appetite slowly return after the dampening effect of their raking over the past together. She took another piece of pizza and another mouthful of wine.

'What is this?' she asked a few minutes later, as music jangled into the room.

'The sound track from the movie *Shrek*,' he said, and brought her the cover.

She looked at the artwork, featuring a big green ogre, a talking donkey, an egotistical prince and a no-nonsense princess. She'd seen the movie a couple of years earlier, and remembered it well. Cute. Clever. Funny. She saw a lot of movies—rental videos that she put on in the middle of the night when she couldn't wind down after a call-out or a busy day. 'Is there a subtext to your choice?' she asked.

'Not really. I just thought the atmosphere could do with some lightening.' He smiled. 'Why? Do you identify the two of us with any of the characters?'

'Some people think I'm an ogre,' she said.

'In princess form?'

'Just an ogre. You must have heard some comments, in three months.'

'A couple,' he conceded. 'Do you mind?'

'That you've heard comments?'

'That your staff think you're an ogre.'

'Since it keeps them on their toes, no, I don't mind.'

'It does more than that.'

'Yes?' she challenged him. 'What does it do? You've analysed this, have you?'

Oh, lord, why had she asked? She could easily have let it go.

She waited, breath held, for his answer.

He didn't give one. A new track started on the CD, and he said, 'This is my favourite,' as if he'd forgotten her question.

'Mmm, it's nice,' she agreed quickly. Then she actually listened to the words, grew hot and wanted to laugh at herself.

He's not saying that, Nell, she scolded herself inwardly. He's already said there was no subtext to his choice. He's not telling you that you're the one he's loved all along. You need to get some perspective here! He just likes the tune...

'What do you tend to listen to?' he asked.

'Oh, a lot of things...' She remembered, suddenly, how much music had always been a part of what they'd had as teenagers. He used to pick away at the guitar, too, and she found it interesting that he still had one.

They'd even had 'their song'—not a pop hit from the charts of the time, but a 1960s classic that had kept turning up on the radio, for no apparent reason, whenever they sat in his car together. When she'd rented the movie *Notting Hill,* she'd had to fast-forward through Bill Withers singing 'Ain't No Sunshine' because it still brought back too many memories.

She tried to manage a better reply. 'Um, all sorts of things. Rock, classical, jazz, opera. That's one of my favourite things about living alone. If I want to sing along to Tosca at midnight while cleaning my bathroom, there's no one to complain.'

'Not the neighbours?'

'Not on Grafton Street. Those Federation brick walls are solid.'

'But you're not selling?' His eyes twinkled again, reminding her of their secret.

She smiled back at him, feeling her heart lift in an unfamiliar way. 'No, I'm not.' *What* secret? she asked herself impatiently, and added aloud, very briskly, 'I should get going, Bren.'

'Sure.' To her surprise, he didn't argue, just stood up and touched his pocket to check for his keys. Maybe he'd achieved what he wanted from the evening. His baggage was out on the table, and he was satisfied. 'Take the rest of the ham and pineapple with you.'

'No, please, I wouldn't...' She let her hands finish the sentence for her, and got to her feet as well.

Bren followed her to the door, ready to usher her through to his garage. He'd always been well mannered. She felt his hand hover lightly against her lower back just as she reached the door. Even though he wasn't touching her, her body still responded as if he were. Then he stretched around her to grasp the handle, which had the accidental effect of enclosing her in his space, his scent, the promise of his touch.

Her heart began to thud, and she was afraid of what she might betray. In another moment, when he'd opened the door, she would be safe. In the meantime, she wished her hand had reached the round metal knob first. That way, she could have avoided this stupid, helpless reaction to how near he stood.

It took her another five seconds to realise that every one of his movements had been intentional—the same five seconds it took for him to let go of the door, put his hand on her waist and bend to kiss her.

What an idiot she was! Couldn't she have seen it coming? In hindsight, the signals had been there. In hindsight, she'd given a few signals of her own in reply. But it had been so long…

His mouth touched one corner of hers, imprinting her skin with pressure and warmth, then it departed. She had time to think, Oh, good. Just that. And to feel a perverse, painful disappointment because it wasn't so much more. She realised she'd automatically closed her eyes, the way she had when taking her first hot bite of pizza nearly an hour ago, so she opened them, lifted her face a little and this time met his lips full on.

She met his gaze, too—glittering and dark and soft, giving and naked and curious, all at once. 'I'm glad you said yes to dinner,' he said, and every word was a caress against her mouth.

Desire hammered into her, making her stomach roll. After seventeen years, she had Bren Forsythe's arms around her again, his taste in her mouth again, and she couldn't believe that it still overwhelmed her just as it always had. Whatever she might say to herself about this, whatever brakes and blocks she might apply, her body wanted it.

Bren had always kissed sweetly, and he still did— as if kissing was enough, kissing was everything. She might have been able to resist if he'd shown more impatience, more of the selfish, urgent male agenda she'd experienced once or twice with other men. But this sweet laziness, this total sense of satisfaction in the present moment lulled her, and she gave in to the hunger she felt. She was so *right* in his arms, feeling his lips, kissing him back, tasting him, exploring, giving her whole self to him with only her mouth.

She felt his hands slide down to her hips, heavy and warm, then around to meet on the rounded swell of her backside. 'Mmm,' he said, as if her body was the comfortable bed he'd fallen onto after a long day. 'Mmm.' The sound vibrated deep in his chest, and she could feel it against her breasts.

She didn't know where to touch him. Here, on his back, where she wanted to? Her fingers ached to feel those ropy muscles he hadn't had at eighteen. She felt exactly the way she'd felt then—young and full to the brim and awed by the power of what two bodies could do to each other. Surely that should have changed with the years? She was astonished that it hadn't, that she could still feel this so strongly, with the same sense of wonderment.

Dimly, she knew that she must not let herself give in to touching him, so she kept her hands hovering, and it made her arms stiff, set her body in panicky angles that didn't gel with what her mouth was doing.

'Hey!' He'd noticed. He straightened and took his lips from hers, then reached for her hands and brought them to his face, kissing each palm in turn. She closed her eyes and shivered with ecstasy as shock waves of sensation ran up her arms. 'That's better,' he murmured.

'No, it isn't. It has to stop.' She gritted her teeth and tried to twist out of his grip, but he ran his hands up her arms and held her again, backing her against the door with a man's lazy confidence in his own strength.

'Yeah?' he said softly, and she knew that her protest hadn't surprised him. He'd expected it. Just how deeply had he seen into her soul these past three months?

'Yes, Bren,' she answered. She didn't fight. Not yet.

'Got some reasons?'

'I have,' she insisted vaguely. 'Plenty. I can't—Don't make me list them. We're adults, and—'

'Adults do this. Adults are allowed to be attracted to each other like this. They're allowed to explore it in whatever way they want, to see where it could go, because there's a chance it could go somewhere incredible. I'm a free agent, Nell, and if you're not, then you're doing an awfully good job of hiding any involvement.'

'Have you been asking questions around the hospital?' Her voice shook a little.

'I haven't needed to.'

She knew that was true. Her single status must radiate from her like a neon glow, part of her protective armour. 'If I'm single,' it said, 'it's because I want to be.'

That wasn't entirely true.

She sometimes had visions of herself in a relationship—something modern and practical and comfortable and convenient. No children. She'd forfeited that right, she felt, by not standing up to her mother seventeen years ago.

But even if a suitable candidate loomed, she'd always doubted that she'd know how to get from here to there. From alone to together. From self-sufficiency to two halves of a whole. From guilt to forgiveness. Anything she'd tried since Bren—in Newcastle and Sydney, not here—had failed miserably, confirming her own sense that she just wasn't meant for such things.

The panic she felt, with Bren still looming over her, suggested she'd been right to doubt.

'I can't, Bren,' she said.

'"I can't"?' he echoed. 'Not "I don't want to", but, "I can't"?'

'All right. I don't want to.'

'Too late. "I can't" was what you said, and that's different. If you didn't want to, you would have said that.'

'Is this a philosophy lecture?'

'It's an attempt to communicate. You kissed the

way I remembered, Nell. *Exactly* the way I remembered.'

She wanted to tell him that he did, too, that he kissed like a dream, but managed to hold that back at least.

'I didn't think you would,' he went on.

'How did you think I would kiss?'

'Stiffly. Or impatiently, maybe. Without tasting it. The way I've seen you eat at the hospital. As if it's a necessary bodily function, but gives you no pleasure. Instead, you kissed like a woman on the brink.'

'Of…?'

'Life. Love. Faith. Everything. Just the way you were at eighteen.'

'That's what Mum always said. That I was on the brink of everything. That I had my whole life ahead. So many choices.'

'She was right,' Bren said.

'No, she wasn't.' She was certain about that.

'Just because you didn't choose me?' he asked.

She shook her head, unable to answer.

He looked at her, leaning so that his face was only an inch or two from hers. He brushed his forehead across hers, bumping it gently. She let out a ragged sigh, then felt his mouth sear against hers one final time, as brief as the first.

'OK,' he said. 'Inquisition's over. Let me drop you home.'

'Back to the hospital,' she reminded him.

'Home,' he said, opening the door to his garage. 'I'll pick you up in the morning and run you in.'

'Did you think I'd be staying the night?' she blurted.

Bren shot her a glance, letting it rake up and down her body, showing her his desire, arrowing it right to the answering core inside her. 'I wouldn't have said no to an offer.'

'There's no offer.'

He grinned at her. 'Don't be embarrassed to reconsider.'

'There's no offer, Bren.'

Nell sat stiffly in his car, and when they reached the T-junction where he had to choose between her place and the hospital, she insisted he turn in the direction of the hospital so she could pick up her car—pick up her safety and her independence and the shell that protected her.

CHAPTER FOUR

'HERE'S your car,' Bren said, swinging into a parking space right beside it.

'You're going in to see Zach?' Nell asked.

'Yes.' He tucked the corner of his mouth, and shrugged. Nell wasn't the only one who could have trouble letting go. 'I know the unit would have phoned if he wasn't doing well, but I'd like to see him for myself all the same, make sure no one's missed anything.'

'Kerry's very good.'

'His haemoglobin was pretty low, as you'd have seen, and he was very lucky with the liver. If there was some damage we didn't spot, and a tear opens up...'

'I'll come with you.'

'There's no need. The nurses—'

'You just admitted there was no need for you to look at him either, Bren.'

'OK, you've got me there,' he answered lightly.

She didn't appreciate his immediate capitulation, he saw. She was frowning and she'd stiffened markedly since those electric moments between them on the way to his garage. She wasn't going to make anything easy for him. She was going to fight anything he tried.

Just how far would she fight him? Until she got him to wonder why on earth he was still interested? He wouldn't be surprised.

Fortunately, he thrived on a challenge.

Maybe that was one of the things that had been wrong, ultimately, between himself and Liz. It had been too easy, too safe, too tame.

When he and Liz had first met, at twenty-four, during his fifth year of medicine, he'd valued something safe and easy for a change. He'd passed the five-year cancer-free mark, but the battle against the disease had wearied and scarred him. His determination not to postpone his medical studies beyond that one initial year had made his fight even harder.

He hadn't done well in his first– and second-year exams, and had had ground to make up. Liz had been happy to coast along and to let their relationship drift into each new stage over the course of months. None of it had demanded a lot of energy or thought, which had left him plenty to put into his studies and his career plans, as he'd needed to.

But he was thirty-five now, the pace in Glenfallon was slower, and he didn't need to nurture his strength and his energy the way he once had. Yes, a challenge might be just what he craved—the very specific challenge of Nell.

The two of them walked to the stairs side by side and headed up to the intensive care unit on the next level.

'His lids flickered a while ago,' Kerry Smithers reported. She was alone in the cubicle with Zach. Mrs Lloyd wasn't in sight. 'I talked to him for a bit, tried to get something more to happen, but nothing yet.'

'You almost woke up for us, did you, Zach?' Nell asked softly, stepping close to the bedside and bending over their patient. 'That's great! Want to have another try? Want to say hello, or just have a look to see who's pestering you like this? If you want us to leave you alone, tell us, OK?'

She instantly seemed more comfortable than she had this afternoon. Because the mother wasn't here? Or could Bren himself take some credit for relaxing her this evening?

There was no response from Zach.

'You just want to sleep, don't you?' Nell continued. 'How about you wake up later, when it gets light? Say hi to your mum. She'd really like that.' She watched him in silence for a moment, then stepped away and shrugged, her face dropping into its usual mask. 'It'll come.'

'It should,' Bren agreed.

He pulled the chart from the holder at the end of the bed and held it out so they could study it together. The figures looked nice and stable, none of the drop in blood pressure and oxygen level or the raised heart rate that had signalled trouble this afternoon. No internal bleeding, then, which remained Bren's biggest fear. Zach's carbon-dioxide levels weren't too high either. Haemoglobin was holding up.

He pretended that he hadn't taken most of this in at a glance, and kept studying the chart as long as Nell did, enjoying the chance to keep her close. Like this, he could study her profile with a subtle sideways glance, and the way her hair caught the light. He could smell the light fragrance she wore, something cool and not too sweet.

She controlled a sigh and stepped back, somehow ending up with the chart in her hands, although it had started out in his.

'Pretty good,' she said. 'We did well. Thanks, Bren, Kerry.' She bent over the bed again. 'And thanks to you, Zach, you're just doing great. The best. Beating the game. Keep it up, OK?'

'Is his mother still around?' Bren asked Kerry, when he could tear his eyes from Nell's pale, beautiful profile.

'She's gone to make some phone calls,' the tall, cheerful woman answered. 'Back soon, I should think. The news on her husband has improved, thank goodness. He's off the critical list, and his parents are on their way to Sydney. Kristin isn't prepared to leave Zach, but she hated the idea of her husband being so ill with no family support on hand. Actually, here she is now.'

Kristin looked frightened to see two doctors beside her son's bed. 'What's happened?' she asked at once.

'Everything's fine, Mrs Lloyd,' Bren answered.

He felt the way Nell stepped back, both physically and emotionally. She had Zach's chart still in her hands, and used it like a stage prop or a shield, conveying the impression that she was busy, absorbed in calculations, unavailable.

Should he feel flattered that she trusted his people skills enough to leave him with the task of interacting with their patient's mother? Or should he feel angry at the barriers she was once again putting up?

Both, he decided. It was valid to feel both emotions at the same time. Not very comfortable, not very logical, but human beings so often weren't either of those things.

'There have been a couple of things we've been watching for,' he told Kristin, 'and that we'll continue to watch for, but he's really doing well. You might want to keep talking to him, because there are signs that he's almost ready to respond.'

'Oh, he is? Oh, that's wonderful!' She sat down beside the bed. 'Zach? It's Mum. Can you say hi for me?'

They all watched his face again, and the unmistakable flicker of his eyelids brought a strangled cry of relief and delight from his mother. A moment later, they were all looking into a pair of lazy green eyes. He didn't speak, and the eyes soon blinked and closed again, but it was the right sign, the right next step.

'How long before he'll wake up properly?' Mrs Lloyd asked. 'Should I keep talking?'

'Leave it for a little while,' Bren said. 'It could happen at any time now, though. Are you going to stay with him tonight?'

'Definitely.'

'I'll be in here again first thing in the morning,' Bren promised the tired woman.

'It was good to hear that there's better news on your husband, Mrs Lloyd,' Nell said.

As usual, it sounded stiff. Not insincere, but definitely uncomfortable.

Why did she have such trouble? Not because she didn't care. Bren was quite certain of that. He and Nell left the unit together, but didn't speak very much on the way. When they reached the ground floor, he asked, 'Off home now?'

Of course, she wasn't.

'Just going to check on a couple of things in the department,' she told him, and peeled off down the corridor that led to Accident and Emergency before he could find the right way to order her not to.

He stood and watched her until she rounded a corner and disappeared from sight. Her gorgeous body covered the distance in long, purposeful strides, as if she'd consciously attempted to stamp out any suggestion of feminine grace over the years.

She'd redone her hair in the car. Its tightly pinned fold at the back of her head showed no messy evidence that someone had kissed her tonight, but its colour was a bright, gleaming beacon to his gaze.

Bren suspected he would go on feeling Nell's body against his all night, in his imagination and his memory. He would feel that flaming hair running through his fingers, and that pale skin against his lips. Had he ever honestly thought he might feel it in reality? That she might respond to his invitation and stay? No, he hadn't.

And had he made a mistake in forcing the issue so soon?

He rethought that final question at once.

So soon?

Three months.

That wasn't soon. It was overdue, and he had lost time to make up for now.

Bren drove home in a restless state and made tea, drinking it close to the boil so that it almost burned his mouth, prowling his space while he took each big, hot mouthful. Coming back to Glenfallon, knowing that Nell was here, he'd thought that getting to know her again might be a matter of ticking off various boxes.

She was single. Tick.

She still had that sharp mind he'd loved. Tick.

She let him know, in subtle female ways, that she would be open to his pursuit. Tick.

But after boxes one and two, it hadn't been like that at all. He couldn't imagine that Nell would ever willingly surrender herself to a man's interest. There'd never be a tick in box three. She would test him all the way, with her hard, prickly exterior and her challenging lines.

When he'd kissed her tonight, he'd honestly thought that that particular box might get a big, fat cross in it, too.

And that could well have been the end of it, if she'd kissed badly—not just because kissing badly was no fun, but because of what it would have said about the way she'd changed.

If she'd kissed badly, he would have satisfied his curiosity, his sense of unfinished business, his instinctive comparison between what he and Liz had had, what Liz now had with Simon, and what Bren thought he might have had at eighteen with Nell. The experiment would have failed, leaving him free to move on, to find the other things he was looking for here in Glenfallon.

But incredibly Nell *did* kiss the way she used to, and he responded the way he used to, and he had an inkling that if he pushed, if he waited, if he didn't accept tonight's panicky rejection as final, they might both discover that other things were still the way they used to be, too.

He felt angry and frustrated.

Of course he did!

He was human.

And male.

If Nell was going to have regrets, qualms, reservations, couldn't she have had them *afterwards*? When they'd already made earth-shattering love together? Was it too much to ask that the two of them could meet his simple male needs first, and get to her incomprehensible female complexities later?

Putting his empty mug on the sink, he laughed at himself for being such a stubborn hostage to his own physiology. Then he thought again, in almost painful detail, about the way she'd kissed him, and realised what a miracle it was.

Here was a woman who'd obviously been damaged by life somehow—by her choices, by her mother's pressure, and even by the responsibilities of the career she apparently lived for—and yet she still kissed like a starry-eyed and passionate girl, putting her whole soul out there for the right man to catch hold of and treasure.

No wonder life had hurt her. No wonder she'd encased her capacity for strong emotion inside an even stronger shell.

Somewhere beyond the cool, competent façade, however, the old, undamaged Nell must still exist, *did* still exist. Bren intended to find her, if Nell herself would let him. And maybe even if she wouldn't.

'I can't believe it has taken us, what, three months, to find a weekend to do this!' Emma Croft said, coming into the kitchen at Nell's at three o'clock on a Saturday afternoon.

'I can,' Nell drawled. 'When you consider that between us we have four careers, three significant others and four children, all of which take priority over a women-only talk-fest and video marathon, I'm not surprised at all.'

Emma looked around and noted that the house seemed empty apart from Nell and herself. 'I'm the first, I guess,' she said.

'Caroline and Kit should be here soon,' Nell answered. 'Gian had an emergency, so Kit's dropping Bonnie off at her grandmother's. Caroline's at the video store, picking up our selections. Where are your girls this weekend?'

They were Emma's husband Pete's girls, really, but Claire Croft had always been a reluctant, nervous mother, with her share of serious problems, so Pete and Emma were raising the five year old twins now, and Emma had risen to the challenge of loving another man's children as her own. Nell wasn't surprised. She knew that Emma was more than capable of that kind of heroism.

'In Canberra, with Claire and her mother,' Emma answered her.

'And Pete's at a conference? You should have gone with him, and spent your time lazing by a Gold Coast pool while he attended the sessions. You deserve it.'

'I wasn't going to be the one to let the rest of you down. If we'd postponed this again, we just never would have got to do it, Nell.'

'Would that have mattered?' she answered lightly, grating chocolate shavings onto a chocolate sponge cake covered in whipped cream. They'd all elected not to eat a proper meal during tonight's marathon. There'd be a constant procession of indulgent finger foods instead. 'Things are different, now. We're not

the Single Professional Women's Club of Glenfallon
any more, strenuously proving to ourselves that we can
enjoy life without a man.'

'That's not what we were ever about, is it? Which
of us needed to prove that?'

'Not me.' The words came out more sharply than
Nell had intended—possibly because she'd just grated
her thumb knuckle instead of the chocolate, and it
hurt. She sucked it for a moment, then ran it under a
stream of water.

'Well, good,' Emma retorted. 'I didn't either. Which
leaves Caroline and Kit as the strenuous ones. You're
not really accusing them of desperation, are you,
Nell?'

'No, I'm just being…difficult. Cynical. As usual.'
She'd known Emma and Caroline since high school.
No lesser level of friendship could have brought on
the confession she made next. If Kit had been here,
even though Kit was a friend, too, she wouldn't have
said it, because Kit was too new. 'Because I'm the
only one left.'

'So you're strenuous and desperate?'

'Looks like it.'

'Is that how you feel?'

'No, not really.' She closed her eyes. 'But I
am…scared, Emma.' Her throat tightened.

'Scared of being lonely?'

'Scared that I want what you've got after all. I
didn't think I did. I thought I loved my life. I do. I
thought it was…' She hesitated, thought of adding
what I deserved, but substituted 'enough' instead. 'But
I don't want to have to love it all on my own, while
you guys are too busy with your happy ever afters to

have time for me.' She stopped, and laughed. 'Listen to me! Pathetic!'

'Do we blame Caroline for this, Eleanor Cassidy?'

'The baby? I'm thrilled about the baby, and the wedding.' The date had been decided on now, just a couple of weeks away. 'Declan's a treasure. Just ignore me, OK? It'll take me a month or two to adjust roles, but soon I'll be perfect godmother material and completely happy about it.'

She took the grater to the sink and rinsed it out, hoping Emma would pick up on her signal that she didn't want to talk about this any more. The silence behind her sounded thick and thoughtful to her ears, and she held her breath when Emma spoke again.

'So, what's your selection?'

Bren Forsythe. I selected him seventeen years ago.

Emma couldn't possibly mean the question that way.

'Sorry?' Nell said.

'You said Caroline's gone to pick up our selections at the video store. So what's yours?'

'Oh. Oh, right.' Nell laughed, relieved. 'A classic. *Roman Holiday*, with two late greats, Gregory Peck and—'

'Audrey Hepburn,' Emma finished for her. 'That's great, because I've only seen it once, about fifteen years ago, but you can't possibly call it a romance. If I remember, the whole idea is that Audrey's a princess and Gregory's a journalist, and they can't ever get together.'

'That's incredibly romantic,' Nell insisted. 'I'm going to weep buckets. I'm looking forward to it hugely, and I've invested in aloe vera tissues specially for the occasion.'

'What about the happy ending? You're allowed to weep buckets, I agree, but then there has to be a happy ending.'

'OK, what's yours?'

'Well, I thought about *Notting Hill* but I watch that every time it comes on television, so I went in a different direction. *Grosse Pointe Blank*, with Minnie Driver and John Cusack,' Emma said.

'Edgy, violent, all the comedy very *noir*. Is that really a romance?'

'The happy ending cancels out everything else. Those two characters belong together. They just didn't know it ten years ago in high school.'

'You know your rules, I guess. Any idea what Caroline and Kit have chosen?'

'Caroline's going for *Out of Sight* with George Clooney and Jennifer Lopez.'

'Haven't seen it.'

'Neither have I,' Emma said. 'Sexiest locked-together-in-the-trunk-of-a-big-American-car scene ever, apparently.'

'Sexy is a good ingredient.' Nell paused, then drawled, 'George Clooney is a good ingredient, come to think of it.'

Emma laughed. 'And Kit wants us to see something called *Happy, Texas*, which she says is quirky and cute, and gave her some good laughs when she needed them a couple of years ago.'

'In that case, I think we've covered the bases on romance in the movies, whether classic, current or in between. Sexy, funny, weepy, with happy endings all round.'

'*Roman Holiday* does *not* have a happy ending!' Emma protested again.

'I disagree! You don't think there'd be a perfect, wonderful lift in your heart just knowing that the two of you loved each other, even if you couldn't be together? Just the looks Audrey and Gregory give each other…'

'All right, Nell.' Emma gave an exaggerated sigh. 'Royal protocol has changed over the years. Maybe they meet again twenty years later, and she's allowed to marry him after all. *Roman Holiday II*.'

'You're right, Hollywood would do that, wouldn't they?'

They both laughed, then heard a car pulling into the driveway.

It was Kit, with her arms full of 'supplies' for their video marathon—dips and chips, and a bottle of wine. She knew about Caroline's baby by this time. Caroline had phoned Nell yesterday to report on their conversation 'because I know you were concerned, and you gave me good advice'.

Kit was a strong person.

'I'm going to treat it as a good omen,' she'd said.

They all knew she was going into hospital this coming Monday for surgery to clear away the endometrial tissue that was blocking her ovaries and Fallopian tubes and preventing her from conceiving. Bren would be performing the procedure.

Then Kit and Gian were taking a two-week holiday on the Barrier Reef, leaving on Friday. Nell suspected they were probably still hoping to conceive naturally, even though they'd already scheduled a cycle of IVF treatment at a highly regarded clinic in Melbourne next month. Kit didn't want to go back to the clinic in Canberra where she'd received infertility treatment a few years ago.

'Bad memories,' she'd explained to Nell. 'Not that I'm superstitious. I'm not going to let myself think that way. But I did want a change.'

Nell ached for her, guessing the way she must be tying herself in knots, trying not to hope too hard, trying not to count on a pregnancy of her own, trying not to see good and bad omens in every detail of her own life and the lives of her friends.

I'm not the only one who needs a marathon of escapist movies, snack foods and wine, she realised.

She looked at the driveway again, and saw Caroline's car pull in behind Kit's.

'Now we just have to work out what order we're going to watch them in,' she announced, taking charge because that was what she did best. 'We need to start straight away, and not get distracted for two hours with conversation, or we'll be up till three in the morning.'

'Good point,' Kit agreed. 'Caroline probably folds into a heap well before midnight anyhow.'

'And we're *not* pulling names out of a hat. We need the right progression of mood.'

CHAPTER FIVE

AFTER the movie marathon was over on that evening, at just past midnight, four yawning women had all agreed that they should do it again. Suspense thrillers next time, maybe, or their favourite comedies.

'And I'm glad you made us walk around the block between each one, Nell,' Kit had said. 'Otherwise I never would have lasted the distance.'

'I didn't *make* you. I just offered a sensible suggestion.'

'Then you put on your jacket, grabbed your keys and set off. Hard not to follow.'

'Anyway, yes, definitely suspense thrillers next time,' Caroline had said. 'Hopefully I won't sleep through one and a half of them, the way I did tonight! Next time I won't be in the middle of this first-trimester fatigue I'd conveniently forgotten about!'

Nell could have come in with another dampening reply. She'd known there wasn't going to be a next time. Weddings to plan, babies to incubate, medical treatments to undergo, trips away to Ireland and Queensland, weekends on call. Too much would get in the way.

But she hadn't said it, and the four women had hugged each other goodnight and gone home. Now it was Monday morning, and Kit would have gone in for her surgery an hour ago. She was the first name on Bren's list today.

Meanwhile, five days after regaining full consciousness, Zach Lloyd continued to make good progress. The diffuse head injury he'd sustained had resolved well, and there was no evidence of ongoing impairment. He was responding appropriately to questions, and moving his limbs according to instructions. He'd been moved out of Intensive Care and, if all continued to go well, he'd be discharged in a few days.

The news on his father wasn't quite so good. Although David had regained consciousness also, he still had problems with speech, movement and memory, and his internal injuries would require further surgery in the future. His damaged lung wouldn't retain its inflation. At the moment, apparently, his surgeons in Sydney were looking at something called a talc pleurodesis to deal with the problem.

Kristin had had questions about it, which Nell had answered. It was a well-tried procedure and should be successful. It involved lining the space between the lung and the chest wall with powdered magnesium silicate—the substance used as a basis for talc, which would encourage the lung to adhere and stay inflated. Yes, it did sound strange, though, didn't it? Talcum powder was for babies' bottoms, not grown mens' lungs.

Kristin had torn herself away from Zach and left for Sydney this morning, with her sister as a substitute at Zach's bedside. Nell was glad that the family had relatives to call on in this way.

The department was busy today, with the usual post-weekend problems. They saw sporting injuries that hadn't cleared up on their own, the way patients had optimistically hoped they would, and they saw the

effects of over-indulgence in alcohol. Not hangovers—
most people self-medicated for those!—but sprains or
abrasions or other injuries resulting from poor co-
ordination and lowered perception of risk.

Nell hid her impatience and her irritation, and
treated each patient with equal professionalism. Her
habitual cool façade did have its positive side. No one
could ever accuse her of favouring one kind of patient
over another.

Glancing into the waiting area, she saw a thin young
girl standing limply beside her mother at the triage
desk, and a frightened woman in her late twenties
leaning on her husband's arm as she waited her turn.

An instinct stemming from years of experience told
her the woman in her twenties looked like the most
urgent case, but she wouldn't rely on instinct. First, in
any case, she still had to check a child with suspected
concussion, who'd just vomited on the corridor floor,
and a man with chest pain that was probably just in-
digestion, but you always had to make sure.

Nell had been doing this for nearly eleven years.
She'd discovered a zest for the variety and the cutting-
edge drama during her internship and hadn't looked
back. Yes, it was scary, sometimes, to be the first line
of defence. The pace could be intense. The patients
could be ungrateful.

Sometimes they upped and died on you, and you
couldn't do a damn thing about it. Sometimes they
walked out in the middle of your treatment, swearing
at you. You saw tragedy and comedy, life richly af-
firmed and life wilfully thrown away.

But it absorbed her, physically, mentally and emotionally, and here in Glenfallon it gave her a very real

sense that she was part of the life of the entire town.
She didn't care if her staff didn't understand quite how
important all of this was to her. Her reward lay in her
results.

'Dr Cassidy, are you ready to look at Mrs Westway,
in Cubicle Three?' asked one of her most experienced
nurses, Helen Bartram, after Nell had finished talking
to the mother of the concussed little girl.

'Coming now,' she answered. 'What do you think
is going on?'

'She's afraid it's a miscarriage. She's sixteen weeks
pregnant. But the pain's wrong for that. Too much on
the side. Given the pregnancy, it could be a rupture in
the ovary.'

'Could be. Is she febrile?'

'Thirty-nine point six, and nauseous.'

'We'll order an ultrasound and see.' Nell valued
Helen's opinion, but wasn't going to prejudge the
case. Appendicitis was also a strong possibility.

She slid the cubicle's curtain aside and found Mrs
Westway lying on her side with a kidney dish held
ready. Definitely nauseous. She sat up and her shoulders began to heave. Helen stepped forward, and Nell
murmured to her, 'Send her for the ultrasound if I'm
not back,' then left again. No sense in examining the
woman until she'd settled again, and that would take
a few minutes, at least.

There was no one at the nurses' station so she
checked the computer, and found the details of two
more patients already entered in. One was a low-
priority football injury, who should be sitting in his
own doctor's office, not cluttering her department. The
other was someone called Brittney Wallace, who had

to be the pale young girl she'd glimpsed some minutes ago.

No one in Glenfallon over the age of eighteen was called Brittney, Nell mused in passing, just as no one under the age of sixty was called Jean, Joan or June. You could rule out certain medical possibilities purely on the basis of fashions in female names.

'Can I take a look at you now, Brittney?' she said to the sixteen-year-old, arriving in the small paediatric section of the department.

Glancing at a line of notes from the nurse who'd dealt with Brittney thus far, she saw some cryptic phrases suggesting she might not get a lot of co-operation, or the same story from mother and daughter. Should she nudge the mother out of the room? The daughter was looking worse than she had in the waiting area—very pale, with fear in her eyes and dark circles under them.

'I'm sure it's some dreadful stomach bug. That, or appendicitis,' Mrs Wallace said, before her daughter could speak.

No, the appendicitis is going to be Deanna Westway, in Cubicle Three, Nell almost said.

She didn't think this one was appendicitis. The symptoms didn't fit, and the patient wasn't co-operative. She admitted to terrible diarrhoea, without vomiting, but there was something else she wasn't saying. Nell managed to get the mother out of the room, then she pushed harder and got the truth.

It added up to the fact that Brittney was, to put it bluntly, three months pregnant, terrified and clueless. She'd taken a barrage of laxatives, drunk half a bottle

of gin and given herself a scalding hot bath in a mis-
guided attempt to bring on a miscarriage.

She'd also taken a big dose of a popular non-
prescription painkiller, and this concerned Nell more
at the moment. Those tablets were fine at the right
dose, but they could cause liver failure if taken to ex-
cess.

She felt Brittney's uterus, which was the right size
for the dates the girl had given, and found a good
heartbeat on the Doppler. She could only hope that
these signs of a healthy baby would be confirmed in
six months' time, after delivery. Meanwhile, the gin,
the bath and the effect of the laxative had left the
teenager seriously dehydrated, and there was the state
of that liver to monitor.

Nell filled in some pretty blunt notations on the
chart, ordered a fast infusion of fluid and told
Margaret, 'Get her admitted to Gynae, Postnatal, or
anywhere there's a bed. She's going to need to be
watched pretty closely for the next twenty-four hours.'

Margaret clicked her tongue and opened her mouth
to editorialise. Nell sighed. 'Save it, Margaret.' In case
that didn't get the message across, she wheeled around
and left without saying anything more.

Back in cubicle three, she found that Deanna
Westway had been sent for her ultrasound. Her tem-
perature had risen to 39.8, now. The nausea had sub-
sided, but the pain hadn't. The right groin was extremely tender on palpation. Helen had taken blood,
and they'd get the result on the white cell count soon.
A raised count could confirm that something—ovary
or appendix—had already ruptured.

Deanna came back twenty minutes later with their

second possible diagnosis confirmed. Her appendix appeared big, juicy and inflamed Possibly ruptured, but only surgery could tell them that for certain.

Not good news. She knew Helen had prepared the Westways for the news that surgery might be necessary, but Nell herself was the one who'd have to sketch out the possible consequences. Might as well get it over with.

'You'll need to have your appendix removed, Mrs Westway,' she said simply. She didn't sketch out the aggressive approach that would be needed if it had already ruptured.

'Is that safe for the baby?' Gavin Westway said. He'd hit on the issue that counted for all of them.

'Safer than doing nothing,' Nell told him. It was true, but it was only half the story. 'Because then the appendix would rupture.' If it hasn't already, she added inwardly. 'And the infection would spread through the entire peritoneal cavity.'

'That doesn't sound good…' Mrs Westway said.

'No. We can't let it go. I'm sorry.' She took a breath. 'Operating at this point in your pregnancy, however, there is a risk of miscarriage.'

'Oh. I knew it. I knew it couldn't be good,' the woman whispered.

'I'm sorry,' Nell answered automatically once again. 'We'll do the best we can to keep you rested and keep the pregnancy going, but I'm not going to make a promise we might not be able to honour.'

Gavin squeezed his wife's hand and they both nodded. Deanna said, 'If we do lose the baby…'

Nell mentally noted the way she'd said 'we.' This

was a wanted child. Well, that had been obvious from the beginning.

'Will it happen straight away?'

More hard news.

'Not necessarily,' she had to say. 'You won't be able to breathe easy for about two weeks. I know that'll probably make it the longest two weeks of your life. It will pass. Meanwhile, try to get comfortable, and I'll give you the news on the surgery as soon as I can. We're not going to delay on this one.'

She left the couple alone, then ran into Bren in the corridor. Right into him, hard into his chest, his knee knocking against her leg. She hadn't even seen him. She'd been too busy pondering the irony of Brittney Wallace doing her foolish best to get rid of an unwanted pregnancy with a barrage of laxatives, painkillers, hot water and gin, instead of opting for a safe, clinical termination, while Deanna Westway might struggle to keep the baby she did want so very much.

'Whoops,' Bren said, grabbing her elbows to steady both of them.

'Sorry,' she gasped.

He wasn't sorry. That smile of his gave his attitude away—the smile that glowed in his eyes and only just touched his mouth, hinting at shared secrets. She could feel his warmth still pressing into her, as they stood thigh to thigh.

'I'm OK now,' she told him. 'You can let go.'

He did, but he turned it into a caress, letting his fingers slide down her arms, squeezing her hands in his, reminding her very deliberately of the way she'd responded to his kiss last week.

'I came to tell you about Kit Di Luzio's surgery,' he said.

'All done?' After a busy morning, Nell had almost forgotten. She stepped back and brushed at her white coat, as if his touch had rumpled it. She knew he would pick up on the nervous gesture, and undoubtedly interpret it with perfect accuracy.

'Yes, the best we could,' he said. 'I've already phoned Gian, who was nice enough not to say that he wished they'd gone somewhere else for the procedure.'

'You think somewhere else could have done it better?'

'No, I don't. Not really. But she has endometrial tissue all over the place, and I don't see her conceiving naturally. I hope she conceives with IVF, because pregnancy and breast-feeding might be the best way to keep her endometriosis under control, at least for a time.'

'Hmm. It doesn't always work that way, does it? They want a child together, not a false cure for her disease. Do you think they have a chance?'

'If they do, it'll be in their first cycle, when the uterus is still relatively clear. After that, of course, the odds diminish the more new tissue builds up. Rotten for both of them.'

Nell nodded, but didn't quite trust herself to speak.

'Do you think she'll handle it?' Bren persisted.

'She'll have to.' And I'm not going to cry about it now. Later I might. 'Meanwhile, I've got an acute appendicitis case for you, sixteen weeks pregnant.'

'Ship 'em in, ship 'em out,' he said, mocking her tone and her attitude. He leaned a hand on the corridor

wall, effectively blocking her escape. She felt en-
closed—not by him but by the treacherous web of sensation her own body had created. 'We run a stream-
lined operation here,' he finished. 'No words wasted
on sympathy.'

'Exactly,' she answered. She wouldn't rise to this
particular bait. 'I save all my sympathy up for weekends.'

'How about this weekend?'

'For sympathy?'

'A pity party for two,' he said. 'Interested?'

'No, since you have to be joking.'

'About the pity party, of course I am, but how about
just—'

'Didn't I already say no to this? Not to the weekend,' she added quickly, before he could make some
pseudo-innocent protest that the subject of the weekend hadn't come up until just this minute. 'but to—'

'This. I know. *This*,' he mimicked. 'One word, Nell,
and we both know what we mean by it. It shafts right
into us. Don't you think that's significant? Worth exploring?'

'No. Anyone would know what we meant by *this*.'

'Would they?' He shifted his hand an inch in her
direction on the wall. His body moved more than an
inch towards hers.

'Yes!' she said.

'What do you mean by it?'

'You know. You just said you did.'

'And you just said anyone would,' he said. 'But
that's not true. People have wildly divergent ideas
about *this*. One-night stand? Convenient affair? True
love? I've heard the expression ''bed buddies'' a cou-

ple of times recently. Is that what *this* is? Are you looking for a bed buddy, Nell?' His dark eyes swam with their usual light, this time mocking her a little, not soft and tender at all.

'No,' she said.

'What are you looking for, then? And don't tell me you're looking for me to back off, because you wouldn't have kissed me…' He dropped his voice and dropped his gaze to her mouth. 'Correction. You *couldn't* have kissed me the way you did the other night if you'd wanted that. So fiery and sweet and real. Look, you're remembering it now, I can tell…'

She was. Low inside her, something swelled and pulsed. Her breathing wasn't quite steady. Her blood heated, suffusing her face with colour that she could feel. She wanted to press her fingers there to hide it.

'You kissed me because you wanted to,' he said, his voice even lower, meant only for her. 'I know you, Nell, and you haven't changed that much.'

Nell made a helpless sound in her throat. 'I—I'm not looking to have this kind of conversation in the middle of a hospital corridor, Bren.'

'So we'll have it somewhere else.'

'Not now.'

'On the weekend. Back to square one. But whatever we decide, let's forget the past, start with a clean slate. Make this new. Is that such a bad idea? Is it so impossible? Even if it ends as just a professional friendship. I'll phone you, OK?'

'Only if it's about a patient, please.' She did her best and most thoroughly practised ice-queen voice, but she knew he wasn't fooled.

For the moment, however, he seemed prepared to

let it go. They both had work to do after all. 'Tell me about the patient we have now,' he said. 'The appendicectomy.'

'We've confirmed it by ultrasound. Don't have a white cell count yet, but it may be ruptured. It's not a good point in her pregnancy for this to be happening, and she's pretty upset. Let's get her into Theatre as soon as we can.'

'And I'll phone you about the weekend tonight or tomorrow. Don't argue, Nell, because one of your nurses is coming down the corridor, and I suspect you'd mind being overheard in a private conversation a lot more than I would.'

'That's probably true,' she agreed tightly.

For the rest of the day, she wondered what his next move would be if she simply didn't answer the phone.

CHAPTER SIX

'IT HADN'T ruptured,' Bren told Nell, when he emerged from Deanna Westway's surgery. 'But it wasn't far off. Swollen and very ugly.'

'And the baby?'

'Holding on. I could see movement, and there was a good heartbeat. Now it's just a matter of waiting.'

Nell was still waiting on her other pregnant patient, too—Brittney Wallace. There wasn't a lot more they could do. The liver either repaired itself, or it didn't. Fluid infusion would prop up the body's own resources, but couldn't be labelled a cure. Brittney didn't seem fully aware of how serious this all was…but, then, to be fair, Nell hadn't spelled it out.

Kindness on her part?

Her staff would laugh at that idea, and they'd be right.

No, it was more cynical than that. She just didn't feel there would be much point.

She arrived home at nine that night, after padding out a couple of quieter afternoon hours in the department with unnecessary catch-up work, so that she could more genuinely look flat out and run off her feet in the evening. She'd grown wise to her own tricks over the years, but if anyone else had caught her at it, they'd never challenged her.

A ten-year-old boy had come to her rescue at around six, and had made the run-off-her-feet performance look more genuine with his failed attempt to jump down an entire flight of concrete stairs.

He'd fractured the end of his tibia and, after studying the X-rays, she'd decided on a lower leg cast rather than the wrap-around splint and bandage she would have used for an adult. Most kids just couldn't stay still, or keep themselves from using the leg, and the bandage and splint would unfasten in no time. The cast would be safer.

'How many steps were you aiming for?' she'd asked Tom Richards.

'Twelve.' He'd been ashamed of himself and proud about it at the same time.

'Someone dared you, right?'

'Alex, my cousin.'

'And how far did you get?'

'Eleven. I almost made it.'

'Grow a few inches before you try it again, OK, Tom?'

He'd grinned sheepishly. 'OK. Mum says I'm not ever allowed to try it again.'

'Yeah, OK, she's right. That's an even better plan.'

Remembering young Tom's attitude, as she peered into her discouraging fridge at home, she grinned, too.

If she had to pick a favourite age group and gender amongst her patients, it would have to be school-age pre-teen boys, like Tom or Zach. They didn't want too much emotion or too much sympathy. Just a bit, given with a light hand.

She could tease them a little, and smile, and not get ambushed by the tight throat and pricking eyes she hated. She felt as if she understood the simple things that were important to them and made them tick. And they injured themselves in such entertaining and ridiculous ways!

Right Now. Dinner.

The possibilities were unimpressive. She found a slice of sponge cake left over from Saturday, but it was dried out around the edges because she hadn't put the lid of the container on properly. She located a couple of remnants of cheese in a similar state. There was also a smear of sour cream and onion dip.

'I know. You're right. I must shop,' she told the fridge. 'But that doesn't solve tonight.'

The supermarket had extended hours. She should have called in there on the way home. She could even get back in the car and go there now, but...

Pizza.

Ten-year-old boys and bachelor surgeons would want pizza on an empty stomach at this time of night, even if they'd had it last Tuesday, too. Hot, salty pizza, just a phone call away, and eaten straight from the box. No dishes to do, no effort to make and, above all, no guilt.

And why not? She didn't have to punish herself like this. It was ridiculous that she had nothing in the fridge, and that she so frequently ended up eating something cold or dry because she'd backed herself into a nutritional corner and at some inner level of her consciousness apparently believed it was where she deserved to be.

She found the phone book and looked up the pizza restaurant, and someone answered and asked her, 'Pick-up or delivery?'

She answered, 'Delivery, please,' with a dawning sense of entitlement and pleasure, and the unsettling realisation that she may just have embarked on a whole new chapter in her life.

The phone rang again less than a minute after she'd put it down, and she picked it up instinctively, vaguely thinking it would be the pizza place confirming her address, or something. She didn't know much about commitment issues between fast-food restaurants and their clientele.

'About the weekend,' said Bren, at the other end of the line.

She answered quickly, 'I've only just got home,' as if she would need at least an hour to get organised before she could possibly think five days ahead.

'Your line was busy a minute ago.'

'It was a short call.' She wasn't going to admit to the pizza. He might guess that he was partially responsible for it. 'Bren, I didn't agree that anything would happen on the weekend.'

'I know. That's why I'm calling. So we've got time to discuss it properly.'

'Is there anything to discuss?' She didn't really know why she was pushing him away like this, except that she was scared.

Maybe that was enough of a reason.

She was scared.

It was a huge reason!

Scared and still suffering.

Would he guess?

'You tell me,' he said. 'I'm hoping there isn't. I'm hoping you'll just agree that it would be good to see each other. A first step towards something. And then we can just decide on a place and a time and get off the phone.'

'I'm on back-up call all weekend.'

'And how often do you write the roster so that you're not on call all weekend, Nell?' he asked her sweetly.

'That's not fair! You know the answer to that. You know I give people like Pete Croft and Alison Cairns a good turn at it so they can keep their skills in hand.'

'While wishing you didn't have to. You should roster yourself one weekend in three, at the most. And even for back-up call you should—'

'Remind me why you're proposing to get together on the weekend,' she cut in. 'To bully me about my schedule?'

Bren laughed, then said much more soberly, 'Would you like to phone me back some time in the next few days? When you've had a chance to think about it?'

Now he was treating her like a child who didn't know her own mind.

And he was right.

Nell felt foolish. Did she really need the masterful treatment? They were equals.

No.

At the moment they weren't.

He held the upper hand because he apparently knew what he wanted.

Her.

Unlikely as that seemed.

Whereas she was a mess and didn't know what she wanted at all. Or what she'd let herself have. Pizza was one thing. Bren was different.

Wasn't he?

She took a deep breath. 'Um, could I, Bren? I— You're right. You were right today. I kissed you back the other night, and it was, well, nice. Wonderful. But there are…other issues I have to consider.'

What other issues?

Fear?

Yes, fear!

She couldn't admit to it.

'Let me phone you later in the week,' she told him.

'Sure,' he said simply, with too much kindness. It made his voice drop, and she heard a husky note in it that almost made her cry. 'Sure, Nell, if that would help.'

She had to wait a moment before she could answer. 'I—I think it would. And so would that thing you said about starting with a clean slate, whether it's a professional friendship, or…something else.'

'OK, we'll go with that, too, then.'

Her skin was burning all over a few seconds later when she put down the phone.

She wandered into the bathroom and looked at her reflection in the mirror.

Hi, Nell.

Blue eyes, tired skin that was too pale, hair that she liked to keep out of trouble. She tried smiling.

Hi, Nell!

Ugh…

The smile looked panicky and forced, nothing like Bren's smile, with its secret heat and understanding.

She reached up and took the pins out of her hair. Oh, that felt good! A couple of them had been pinching and pulling, and she hadn't even realised. Her hair tumbled down around her face, alarming in the way it changed her appearance. Shadowed by the loose waves, her skin didn't look so bad after all, and her eyes seemed darker.

Frowning at herself, she thought about the incredible fact that Bren wanted to start again, to try again. The two of them. She'd be a fool to keep fighting him, wouldn't she? She should walk forward and meet this, with courage. *This.* He'd challenged her use of the word, demanding a more accurate definition. She didn't need a definition from him.

He came from a close, loving family, and his parents were apparently still together, after nearly forty years. Reading between the lines, she was certain that he'd never been unfaithful to a woman he'd been involved with, and that he never would be. She knew he would be looking for a relationship that meant something, whether it lasted three months or a lifetime, and that if he didn't find it with her, it wouldn't be because he'd taken the whole thing too lightly.

The ball was in her court.

The doorbell rang. Her pizza. Mmm! Her stomach growled in impatient anticipation. She grabbed her bag, got out some cash and hurried to the door, and as she took the white box into her hands and smelled the aroma that rose from it, reminding her of last week, and Bren, she decided, yes, I'll do this.

Ignore the fear, Nell.

Start again.

Try, at least.

'You've been lucky,' Nell said to Brittney the next morning in the gynaecology ward, where a bed had been found for the sixteen-year-old.

Brittney nodded at Nell's words, but Nell wasn't convinced she'd got the message across.

She drove it home a little harder, inwardly asking herself the same question she'd asked yesterday. Was she being cynical here, or kind?

'It's extremely improbable that what you did would have caused a healthy pregnancy to miscarry,' she said, 'but you could have destroyed your liver. And you could have damaged your baby.'

'I'm sorry,' Brittney whispered.

Nell softened her voice a fraction. 'Don't apologise, Brittney. Look, I'm not yelling at you, and I'm not the one you should apologise to. You just need to be clear on what you want.'

'I—OK. I know that now.'

'If you really, seriously don't want this baby, then we can help you arrange for a proper, safe termination, performed by a doctor under the right conditions. If that's not what you want, you must nurture and nourish this pregnancy for the baby's sake, and make up your mind between adoption and keeping it yourself.'

'I want to keep it myself. Mum says she'll help.'

'That's good. It's good to reach a decision, and to know you'll have support.'

I hope you're grateful for it, she wanted to add, but didn't.

If ten-year-old boys were her favourite patients, teenage girls with accidental pregnancies were the ones she liked to deal with least. She empathised with them too much, and understood their fears and their complex emotions too well—which meant, of course, that empathy was the very last emotion she ever let herself show.

What would happen if, for once, she responded differently?

Pausing in the doorway of Brittney's room, she turned back to the teenager and added more gently, 'I know this is a terribly difficult time for you, and you've felt very alone. It's been hard to think clearly, and make good decisions. Even if you can't always communicate well with your parents, or they're not reacting the way you need, there are counselling services available. You're *not* alone. Try and remember that.'

Brittney nodded again.

Nell gave herself a tiny handful of points for trying. Two. The points she'd have got in a magazine quiz for answering choice (b).

Back in her department, she found another mother and daughter pair, but this time the mother was the patient and the daughter the person who'd brought her in. The elderly woman had severe left-side abdominal pain, tender to the touch, and a history that set off alarm bells for Nell as soon as she got part-way into her examination and questions.

A section of the sigmoid colon had ruptured, it turned out, and that meant more emergency surgery for Bren. They exchanged the necessary information, while Margaret prepped the patient for her operation. The wheeled stretcher trundled off along the corridor in the hands of orderly Andy Fairbrother. Bren was about to follow, but Nell put a hand on his arm and he stilled at once and looked at her.

'I was going to phone,' she said, 'but since we have a moment...'

'Yes?' He looked wary, ready for anything.

Nell felt a ridiculous lurch of fear in the pit of her stomach. She ignored it and told him, 'I wanted to say yes to the weekend.'

He gave a tiny nod. 'Good.'

Just that?

Well, what had she expected, in a hospital corridor?

All the same, her stomach lurched again, and she rattled on impulsively, 'I'm not sure what you had in mind, but I wondered if you'd be interested in coming out to Dad's farm with me and looking at his bees? We only need stay as long as we want, then we can do something else. I know you were kidding about the bee-keeping thing the other night, but it is fun, and—'

'And you want to avoid that first-date feeling of staring across a restaurant table at each other, right?' he muttered, smiling.

'Something like that.' She smiled back, relieved.

'What time? Shall I pick you up? I'll drive, and you can tell me where to go.'

'Elevenish, Saturday? Give the town time to wake up first, and decide if they need to visit my department for a quick episode of life-threatening drama.'

He laughed. 'That would be pretty typical, wouldn't it? Maybe now you've predicted it, it won't happen.'

'Do you operate that way, Bren? Do you take an umbrella when you particularly don't want it to rain?'

'Well, lately I've tried over-watering the plants on my front porch to get it to rain and break the drought, but it hasn't worked.'

'We need more brides planning outdoor weddings, perhaps.' Oh, gosh, stop it, Nell! Relax! Save it for the weekend! 'Um, update me on the surgery as soon as you can, won't you? We haven't had anything like this for a long time.'

'I have, though, in Melbourne,' he answered. 'She looked pretty strong, and Pete's good on anaesthesia. It'll depend on the size of the tear, and how quickly we can get in and out. Is the daughter waiting?'

'No, she's going to come back later.'

'See you on the weekend, then.'

'You'll see me a lot sooner than that!'

'I know.' His eyes smiled, and his mouth teased. 'But the weekend is what I'm looking forward to.'

Nell was looking forward to the weekend also.

Stupidly. Dangerously.

The rest of the week passed. Brittney Wallace's liver stayed problem-free and her body rehydrated. She was discharged, her baby's heart still beating strongly, with an appointment already made to see Pete Croft for her initial antenatal care. Zach Lloyd was discharged as well, while elderly Mrs Osterman survived the removal of her sigmoid colon and began to make a good recovery.

Nell went home early on Wednesday—at six—and cooked herself a mushroom and cheese omelette for her evening meal, with a pre-mixed bag of gourmet salad greens on the side. On Thursday, she went home early again, and got take-away Thai food, enough to last for Friday's dinner as well. To her surprise, the little red needle on her mental guilt-o-meter barely gave a flicker above zero.

On Saturday, she was ready and waiting for Bren at eleven, when his car turned into her driveway. The weather was warm and sunny for the first weekend of spring, which meant that her father would be starting to open and check his hives. She'd put on jeans and a pink top that clashed in a satisfying way with her hair. She had her mobile phone in her pocket but it hadn't uttered a sound yet, and she'd started to hope it might not. Or not for a few hours, anyway.

She even felt calm—almost—about seeing Bren, going out, having an open-ended day, until he said to her as he walked her back to his car, 'So, how does your dad feel about playing chaperon today?'

It hadn't even occurred to her that this was what she'd done in making that impulsive suggestion on Monday. Now she didn't understand how she could have been so blind. She'd set up a situation in which two thirty-five-year-old adults, living in a democratic western society in the twenty-first century, would be conducting their first clean-slate date in seventeen years under the eye of one of their parents.

She gasped as the realisation hit, and Bren laughed. 'Didn't you think about that?'

'No. I—How stupid!'

'Don't beat yourself up about it. I remember him. He's nice.'

'He is.' And a lot happier since his divorce from Mum. They'd never been very well suited. 'That's not the point.'

Bren leaned his elbow on the steering-wheel, nuzzled his cheek against his knuckles in an absent-minded way and asked, 'Should I kiss you now, then, when he's not around? That way, we won't be thinking about it all day while we're tasting honey.'

'Bren, if you kiss me now, we'll be thinking about it even more,' she blurted, then looked at him. Glared, actually. 'You *like* doing this, don't you? You like making me say things I regret as soon as they're out of my mouth.'

'Mmm, does have its fun moments, I admit,' he murmured, mouth serious, eyes smiling. 'So can I have that kiss, then?'

'Yes,' she almost yelled. 'Sure. Here. Take it.'

She dived at him, landing her arm against his shoulder. He put out a hand to fend her off the gearstick that jutted up between their two seats, then let it drop to her thigh. 'Hang on,' he said. 'No hurry. Let's do it right.' He brushed her hair back from her face. 'I like this today, not so high and tight.'

She'd pulled bits of it back on each side with a couple of plain clips, but had left most of it loose. In the hope that Bren would do exactly what he was doing, probably—stroke the strands, and run his fingers through them.

He leaned a little closer. 'I like your top, too. The way it yells at your hair. The way it fits. The way it's open around the neck. You have such lovely skin.'

'Too pale.'

'No.'

He touched her just below her ear, then stroked his fingers down to her shoulder. His cheek came to rest against hers—so warm!—and she closed her eyes and drank in the scent of him, fresh and musky. Instinctively, she turned her head in his direction, like a blind creature seeking the light, and he turned, too.

Their lips met softly, barely moving, lazy. He tasted faintly of coffee, of toothpaste, and of himself. Nell felt her hunger for him surge like a wall of floodwater in a narrow ravine. It was so delightful, so wonderful, she just couldn't think about anything else, even the fact that she was afraid.

Last week, she hadn't let herself touch him. Today, she couldn't keep her hands away. She rested them on his upper thighs, knowing how this would arouse him and wanting it, wanting to feel him shudder and wrap his arms around her more tightly, wanting to hear him groan her name.

'You were right,' he said, branding her mouth with every word. 'We will think about it even more. Too late to go back now.'

'Back?'

'To not having kissed this morning.'

She laughed and curved her palms over his jaw. 'You say some funny things.'

'So do you. Like suggesting we go out to your father's and look at bees.'

'You could have said no.'

'I took what was offered. Anyway, I'm teasing. Let's go and see bees.'

'OK.' She felt breathless, as expectant and giddy as the teenager she'd been seventeen years ago. Couldn't help thinking about it, remembering and making the comparison, despite the clean slate they'd decided on.

They drove through the centre of town and stopped at the Glenfallon Bakery for a long stick of crusty French bread. 'Our contribution to lunch?' Bren asked.

'Not exactly. Dad keeps his pantry well stocked and I usually cook something for us when I'm out there.' She was far better at cooking for other people than for herself, in fact. She'd sort of known this already, but saw it in a new light today. She went on, 'No, the bread is for honey tasting. Dad loves to have someone new to try out his different batches on. He treats it like wine.'

'Am I going to have to talk about peach accents and citrus notes, as if I was quoting from a wine label, then?'

'You wait!'

Nell always enjoyed the drive out towards the Carrawirra Hills, past citrus groves and vineyards, with the more arid sheep country in the distance. Dad's acreage was poised between the two, and he had orchard trees and flowers in an irrigated section, and stands of eucalyptus and other natives on the drier slopes.

He claimed that the bees existed to pollinate the trees and shrubs, but Nell secretly knew it was the other way around. He'd planted the vegetation to feed the bees, and give variety to the flavours of his honey.

She directed Bren off the main road and along the kilometre of corrugated dirt that led to her father's. The house was very modest—a weatherboard and fibro construction dating from the 1930s, known in Australia as a 'Tocumwal'.

Dad didn't seem to mind such a simple dwelling. He had big trees hanging over it for shade in summer, a slow combustion stove for warmth in winter, a study for all his books on gardening and geology and bees, and another room lined with carefully labelled shelves where he stored his honey and wax, and he lived out of doors as much as possible.

He'd turned sixty earlier in the year. Nell knew that one day she'd have to insist that he move back into town to live with her, but she hoped that wouldn't be for another fifteen years at least. He was healthy, and she ordered him to the doctor for regular check-ups and nagged him like a fussy parent about hats and sunscreen.

'Park here in the shade,' she told Bren, indicating the big pepper trees that had to be at least forty years old.

Her father had heard the car, and came out to meet them. Nell held her breath for a moment. Dad had stood back from the arguments and tears she and Mum had engaged in seventeen years ago. She suspected he'd simply felt helpless. He'd wanted to take her side, the way he so often did, but on that occasion he hadn't known how to do it, or what 'her side' was. In the end, he'd told her reluctantly, 'I think your mother is right.'

She still didn't know if that was true, but she knew he must remember Bren, and remember exactly who he was.

The cause of all the trouble, according to Mum.

'Bren,' he said, and stuck out his hand, which Bren took. 'Ready? I've got a bee suit that should fit you in the laundry. You'll need to cover up that dark shirt. They don't like dark colours.'

Nell began to breathe again, and hid a smile. She should have known it would be all right. Dad's bees and his enthusiasm for them could camouflage the most awkward of social encounters.

They entered the house and she found her own white bee suit, her boots, gloves, hat and net in their usual place on a shelf in the laundry, and took them into Dad's bedroom to put them on, leaving the bread on the kitchen countertop in passing. Bren changed in the bathroom, while Dad climbed into his gear in the open air, at the foot of the back steps.

The three of them met up a few minutes later. Dad had his smoke pot chugging gently in his hand, his hive tool in its special pocket on his overalls, and his wax container ready. They spent an hour with the bees, opening up two of the hives and inspecting their contents, while Dad gave a running commentary of bee information.

'Bee space, it's called—nine millimetres between each comb. Bees use the energy from eight grams of honey to produce one gram of wax. In terms of bee labour, that makes it quite valuable. That's why we keep even these small amounts, to render and purify.'

'How's that done?' Bren asked.

He seemed genuinely interested. Nell kept peeping at him through her net—better than sunglasses for disguising what you were looking at. She felt shy, and oddly anxious that the two of them should get on, respect each other, not fall into misunderstandings or run out of things to say.

'Well, the melting point of beeswax is very low. Just sixty-four degrees centigrade. Big commercial beekeepers will use more complex equipment for rendering, but I like my little solar contraption.'

'Are you using that today?'

'I could, if you'd like to see how it works. It won't go as fast as it does in summer, but there's enough heat in the sun now.'

'That'd be great.'

'We'll set it going, do some tasting, then have lunch. Quick barbecue, Nell? I've got some kebab sticks and sausages we could defrost in the micro-wave.'

'That'd be nice, Dad.'

'Want to slice up some bread for our tasting?'

'Just let me get out of my gear.'

They tasted clover and yellow box and lavender honeys, smeared on thinly sliced rounds of bread. Bren commented, 'I didn't realise they'd taste so different. I always thought it must be a bit of a gimmick, to claim that bees gathering from one kind of flower would yield a different flavoured honey from those who gathered from another kind.'

'Oh, it's no gimmick,' Dad assured him earnestly. 'Ready for something a bit more adventurous? You didn't know honey could be adventurous, did you?'

'Dad...' Nell said, laughing.

'It's OK, love. You're interested, aren't you, Bren? Try this. Fennel. A lot of people don't like the aniseed flavour, but I'm quite fond of it now.'

'Mmm, it's different, isn't it?'

'There's a big range in the colour, too, have you noticed? The yellow box honey is quite light, while this blue gum honey is much darker.'

Nell left them alone and went to turn on the bar-becue that sat on the back veranda. There were salad ingredients in the fridge, and she sliced some onion to fry as well. She felt good, relaxed, content. Dad's place, and his company, always had this effect on her. He didn't make the demands on her that Mum still did.

She hadn't been up to Queensland to see her mother in ages, she realised, not since Mum's move to her new unit, overlooking the river. It was probably time to plan a visit. She felt the usual reluctance settle over her like a damp blanket, and found the courage to examine the feeling. Mum would, no doubt, call her to account as usual, and suggest a career-enhancing move to the city.

'Don't worry about your father,' Mum might say. 'If he's chosen to fritter away his days, that's his problem. You don't owe him a companionship that he's too ineffectual to look for himself.'

It's time I was firmer with her, Nell decided.

Not unpleasant or hurtful, just firm.

And there are questions I want to ask her, too...

'Time to put on the meat?' Dad asked. He stomped over to the sink, still wearing his bee boots, and washed his hands.

Bren did the same, and they both went out to put the meat on the grill. Guessing what Dad's next request would be, Nell followed them, carrying two beers and a mix of white wine, lime cordial and soda water for herself.

Dad insisted that she and Bren should sit while he presided over the meat, and they talked about the drought, local salination problems, Bren's work and Nell's. Dad asked most of the questions, and showed the same interest in the answers as he assumed others would show on the subject of his bees.

When they'd finished eating, he said, 'I'll clear this lot up later. Bren, did you want to see if we've got some wax?'

Dad had positioned his home-made solar wax extractor to face the sun, whose rays had been intensified by the double-glazed lid. The melted wax had run down the sloping back interior of the box, through a filter, to collect in a metal trough at the bottom.

'It'll harden when I bring it inside. Most of the impurities are left behind in the box, or in the filter. Anything that's left will settle to the bottom of the block, and I can scrape it off. Simple.'

'Ingenious. You use the wax for candles?'

'I sell it, when there's enough to make it worthwhile. It's used in all sorts of things. Now, you two will want to head off in a minute, won't you? Come and choose your honey, Bren. How many jars would you like? Two? Three? Take whatever you want.'

'You're not giving it to me, are you? I don't want to be responsible for slashing your profit margin.'

Nell laughed. 'How long since you've sold any, Dad?' Knowing the answer, she didn't wait for it but continued, 'He ends up giving it all away, Bren.'

'What would I get for it?' her father protested. 'A few dollars here and there. This way, I know it's going to a good home.'

'He's pretty incredible,' Bren said a few minutes later, in the car.

'I'm glad you thought so. I don't know what I'd do without him.'

A rare note of emotion jarred Nell's voice, and Bren thought that most people at Glenfallon Hospital wouldn't recognise this woman as the same one who'd written those 'All staff must...' notices scattered around the A&E department. Even her long-term friends, people like Caroline Archer and Emma Croft, probably hadn't seen this side of her.

'You keep him to yourself, though, don't you?' he

said, and even though he spoke gently, he knew that the words were more of a challenge than a question.

Nell looked at him, her head tilted a little. 'Do I? No, I don't. He has a million friends! Everyone in the local beekeepers' association, and the Rotary club... I couldn't name a quarter of them.'

'Do you ever invite him to lunch at the hospital? Or to dinner at your place?'

'I'd rather go out to him.'

'So you can keep him to yourself,' Bren repeated.

'I just took you there with me.'

'And I appreciate what a rare honour it was.'

'What happened? We were having a nice time until a minute ago.' She gave a short laugh.

'We still are.'

'No, you're interrogating me, and psychoanalysing my answers.'

'I'm sorry.' She had a point, he thought. 'I was...just curious. That's good, Nell—the fact that I'm curious about you, the complexity of you.'

'The enigmatic Eleanor Cassidy?'

'Something like that. Take it as a compliment, OK?'

'I'll try.'

'All right.' He could see that she wasn't convinced. Since they were still juddering along the bumpy farm road at thirty kilometres an hour, it was easy to veer to the side and halt the car. 'Would it be easier for you to take this as a compliment instead?' he asked, his voice charged with intent.

And this time he didn't plan to kiss her gently.

CHAPTER SEVEN

BREN held Nell's face captive in his warm hands.

They still smelled faintly of beeswax and honey—
she could see a tiny, sticky smear on his wrist—and
he tasted just a little of beer. He had to know even
before he touched her lips with his that she would kiss
him back. That was never in doubt, for either of them.

Nell closed her eyes and gave in to everything she
felt. She was giddy with the danger of it, and with the
delight. His mouth seemed so confident and strong,
tasting her, drinking her, pulling her response. His
throat rumbled with a deep, cat-like purr and she
sighed at the sound, put her hands on his hips and
tried to wriggle closer, wanting to feel the vibration
of his voice as well as hear it.

'Too much in the way,' she said.

'Are you analysing, Nell?'

'Analysing? No, the gearstick. The brake.'

He laughed. 'That's what you meant? That's all?
That we can deal with.' He stretched and reached past
her, his weight pushing against her side and her thighs.
She loved the sight of the muscles in his back twisting
as he moved. Near her ankles, he flicked something
and the passenger seat slid back beneath her. 'Can you
scoot over?' he said.

'An inch or two.'

'And up. There.' Somehow he'd slid across and
taken her onto his lap, and she had to lean over him

and kiss him again, because if she didn't, her head bumped the car's ceiling. 'Better?'

Much.

She had to hold her breathing back, hold it steady, as he slid his hands up inside her top. He had a perfect sense of direction. They both knew exactly where he wanted to go, but he took forever to get there—a slow, delicious forever of soft touching and stroking across every inch of tender skin on her stomach and sides.

'Tell me what you're wearing before I touch you there.'

'Lace.'

'Lace…' His hands reached her breasts at last as he spoke the word. The lace was his only barrier, and her nipples furled against the fabric and began to ache. 'What colour?'

'Blue.'

'Pale?'

'Yes.'

'Mmm, blue and red and white.'

'Red?'

'Your nipples, and then your white skin.'

'My nipples are pink.'

'Not after I've taken them in my mouth. They'll darken. You'll have to tell me to stop, or tomorrow they'll feel sore.'

'No…'

'They won't?'

'I won't tell you to stop.'

'Now?'

Now would be crazy, here on this sunny road, but she nodded anyway. 'Yes. Please.'

'Just a taste. A promise. For later.'

He unhooked her bra and she felt it loosen, felt a shifting of weight. He pushed up her top and cupped her breasts in his hands, lifting them and drawing them together. She felt his breath fill the valley he'd created, warm and cool at the same time. Surely that wasn't possible.

'I was right,' he said. 'Red. Not pink.'

A shudder rippled through her as he took each peak, in turn, into the dark heat of his mouth. Yes, she would feel sore tomorrow, and it would remind her delectably of this—of the way her core pulsed and swelled and coiled, of the way her fingers curved at the back of his neck while his mouth took its sweet fill of her.

Finally, she felt a sting of cool air on each wet bud as he lifted his face.

'Problem is, it's too fabulous, Nell,' he said. 'I want more, and where do we go from here?'

'Home,' she said, without a heartbeat's pause.

'Your place?'

'Yes.'

'Now?' His dark eyes searched her face.

'You want to, don't you?' Her nipples throbbed. Her whole body throbbed, and he couldn't pretend that his didn't. 'You do.' She could feel the evidence.

'We're supposed to spin it out a little longer,' he said. 'Go for a wander somewhere, holding hands. Stare at each other over a bottle of wine and wait for it to get dark.'

'I could get called out.' She didn't care how impatient or how calculating it sounded. She'd gone beyond any of that.

So, apparently, had he. 'Let's go to your place. I want you so much, Nell. You're right. If your pager went off, and we'd waited...' He swore, pulled her against him and kissed her with rough hunger, while her top was still bunched to her armpits and her bare, aching breasts grazed his shirt.

Somehow he made it back into the driver's seat, and she used the opportunity to refasten her bra and pull her top down. A car swished by, making the gravel pop and the dust billow. Instinctively, they turned and grinned at each other. Nell's breathing quickened again.

'I'm assuming the glare off the windscreen provides an effective camouflage,' Bren said.

'You positioned the car with that in mind, right?' Her voice sounded fluttery to her own ears.

'The appropriate solar orientation,' he agreed seriously. 'Like your father's wax rendering kit.'

'Two people can stop innocently by the side of the road. We could have been checking the map.'

'I might need to in a minute, Nell. I'm...off the planet. Have to be honest. I'm... Wish your place was closer.'

'You could drive fast.'

He hugged the speed limit all the way, and they stumbled in through her back door, already reaching out for each other again. Afternoon heat and sun filled the bedroom, and Nell left the curtains open. The room looked out into a protective screen of garden greenery, but even if it hadn't, would she have taken the time? Would she have shut out that warm, sensuous sunlight?

No. Not today.

Bren peeled his shirt over his head and flung it on the floor, arresting Nell in the more sedate act of slipping off her shoes. White light etched the outline of his shoulders and his back, gleaming on tiny hairs.

Casting the shoes aside, she came towards him and ran her hands from his neck to his wrists, up to the bare shield of his chest, and around to his back, where the warmth of skin met the warmth of the day and the air. His body seemed blindingly beautiful, hard and brown and male and belonging totally to her.

She unsnapped the front of her jeans and he reached forward and began to pull them down over her hips, helped by the shimmying movement she made. More impatient by the second, she crossed her arms, lifted her pink top, pinched her bra tight at the back and released the hooks, pulled off her briefs.

Still wearing jeans and boots, Bren lifted her nakedness against him, high onto his hips. She wrapped her legs around his waist and felt the tight ridge of cloth and man pushing into her. He buried his face between her breasts, found a nipple and bit her gently.

'Watermelon red, made for my mouth, made for suckling you like this for hours,' he muttered, as if he knew that his words, and the images they conjured, would arouse her even more.

She hadn't made the bed this morning.

Inexcusable. She'd had plenty of time. She just hadn't done it. For some reason, she'd needed to challenge her own disciplined habits lately.

Now, the bed reposed in the room like an invitation, its finely woven cream sheets rumpled and striped with thick shafts of sunlight. With her arms around Bren's neck, Nell released the grip of her thighs around his waist and sank onto the hot, bright expanse, pulling him down on top of her.

He kissed her with sweet, deep heat, covering her mouth, her neck, her shoulders, her breasts, and lower, and lower, tasting her until she was a quivering, molten creature who could hardly remember her own name.

'Nell?' he whispered at last. 'We have to let each other go, so I can—if you want me—because I'm still wearing my…'

'Oh. Oh, yes.' She blinked, laughed, dropped her arms and hugged her shuddering body for a moment.

Bren pivoted so he could sit and take off his boots, and she sat behind him, cradling his back against her chest, wanting him too much and too urgently to let go of him for a second longer than she had to. When he turned back into her arms, he had a small packet in his hand—the only thing that could make a barrier between them now.

A necessary barrier, quickly in place. Neither of them wanted any more waiting.

He filled her like a flood and she cried out, aching and tight around him. When he tried to pace himself, and to hold his weight off her body, she shook her head and pulled him down, wanting the sensation of his whole torso against her, heavy on her, moving.

'This?' he whispered.

'Yes.'

'Now?'

'Yes. Oh, yes, Bren.'

They moved together in a primal rhythm. She felt pulses whip his body from head to toe, and gripped onto him, her own climax reawakening in response to his. Her frantic kisses missed his face and sank into his shoulder and his neck, and they felt like the safest, most beloved places in the world, made just for her mouth, and hers alone.

The two of them lay entwined together for a long time afterwards, their replete bodies caressed by the sun and by folds of sheet fabric that smelled like lemon and fresh air. At some point, they eased apart, but only enough to hold each other, front to back, while they dozed. The light had shifted and turned to gold by the time they woke up again.

'Your pager didn't go off,' he said.

'No, for a miracle.'

'Do you think we could…uh…achieve two miracles in one afternoon?'

She smiled at him, the breath catching in her throat. 'I'd be prepared to try.'

'Mmm, that's what I hoped you'd say…'

Another hour later, they reluctantly dressed, still pager-free.

'But it can't last,' Nell said.

'Superstitious.' Bren stepped towards her.

'You betcha!'

'What do you want to do?' He hooked his chin across the top of her head, put his arms around her, then tilted his face to kiss her, just above her ear.

Nell drew in a deep breath before she answered, purely so that she could fill her lungs with Bren—the smell of his shirt, the feel of tight, bursting happiness and hope that he made inside her. 'If I had to think long term,' she said, 'say, the next half hour…'

'That long term? Wow!'

'I'm really not prepared to go any longer than that.'

'OK. Very sensible.'

'Then I'd say, something to eat? It must be—'

'Seven.' Over her head, he could see the bedside clock radio that kept vigil over her mornings. 'Something to eat would be good. What do you have?'

'Not a lot. Um, at the moment. I…haven't shopped this week.'

'Supermarket's still open,' he pointed out.

'We could do a stir-fry. Quick but nourishing.'

Like this. This was nourishing, and it had been quick. Or *reached quickly* anyhow. It was the same *this* they'd talked about last week. Bren had said that a more exact definition wasn't necessary, but already Nell wondered.

Beyond the intensity of love-making, what came next? She was frightened about the possibilities, and her equating half an hour with 'long term' had a more serious sub-text than Bren had guessed.

'Sounds good,' he answered her, before she'd answered her own silent question about a different kind of *next*.

They shopped like new lovers, stealing kisses and whispers in the aisles, consulting earnestly over each other's preferences as to vegetables and meat. Seasoned couples would shop much more quickly, and without all the negotiations.

Back at her place, Bren suggested wine but she shook her head. 'That pager is still suspiciously silent. Even in Glenfallon, Saturday night can be full on in the emergency department. Well, you'd know. I'm usually called at some point, when I'm on back-up. You have some, though.'

'If you'll take the occasional sip.'

They put on some music and cooked together, and

the meal was ready in half an hour. Nell had taken precisely three bites when her pager did what she'd been expecting it to do for hours. She shovelled in one more mouthful and phoned the hospital while she was still chewing.

Bren found a couple of plastic microwave dishes in one of Nell's big kitchen drawers, and stored the remaining rice and stir-fry in them. He washed the dishes, caught the late news headlines, made some coffee. Nell's car headlights swept across the front living room at five minutes after midnight.

'Overdose,' she said as she stepped inside, her voice brisk and dismissive and tired, her face shuttered.

Watching her peel off her white coat and unhook the stethoscope she'd forgotten to remove at the hospital, Bren was tempted to grill her for detail. Accidental or deliberate? Illicit or licit drug? A cocktail of them, maybe? Good outcome or bad? She'd been a while, so it couldn't have been the relatively simple matter of reversing a heroin hit gone wrong.

No, he decided. Let it go. She's attempting to leave her work behind for once. So let her do it. I can see how hard she's trying. 'Hungry?' he said instead.

'Is there still…?' Her face brightened, but she couldn't even finish the sentence.

'What, you thought I might have taken advantage of your absence and wolfed the lot?'

She laughed. 'No, but it seems so long ago.' She sounded oddly wistful about it. 'And too much trouble.'

'It'll take two minutes in the microwave. You sit.'

'Mmm. Yes, sir!'

'Coffee?'

'Might as well.'

'You think you'll have to go back?'

She shrugged. 'Since I really don't feel like it to-night, that's the most likely thing to happen.'

He slung the rice and the stir-fry in the microwave in their twin containers and left them to their sedate, circular dance, poured a mug of milky coffee and came to sit down beside her. Her matching set of three-seater couch and two armchairs was dusty pink, he'd discovered, and he hadn't known whether to be surprised about this colour selection or not. She'd worn pink today, too.

'Usually, it's hard to keep you away from the place.' He handed her the mug, and covertly watched the way her fingers closed around it, as if she were cold. His body sank deeper into the squishy cushions of the couch, bringing his thigh close against hers. She didn't edge away.

'Distractions at home this weekend,' she said.

'Nice ones, I hope.'

'You're fishing, Forsythe.'

'For information, not ego strokes. I want to know if we can do this again. Now that we've made the initial experiment, and it's been… Well, *has* it been? For you? A success?'

He should sound more fluent than that, he realised. And possibly more masterful. He felt masterful. And impatient. Desire-filled. Aching. Dizzy with achieve-ment. Walking on eggshells.

Would Nell be Nell if she simply dropped into his open hand? He didn't think so. This wasn't going to be as easy as it had so triumphantly seemed at one point—or several points—earlier today. He had to steer a steady course here, even if Nell didn't. Even if she, for some reason that he hadn't worked out yet, *couldn't.*

She nodded in answer and sipped her coffee, narrowing her electric blue eyes against the steam. The microwave pinged. 'You wouldn't believe me if I said no,' she added.

'I might, if you explained.'

'It was a success, Bren.'

She turned her head and looked at him, her face suddenly naked and incredibly vulnerable. His heart flipped and his breath caught. She leaned her cheek into his shoulder and sat there in silence, not drinking her coffee, and the silence was loud, loud, loud. He didn't know what it meant.

'So, want your stir-fry?' he asked, after what must have been several minutes.

'I'll get it. You've been great. I—I didn't know if you'd even still be here.'

'If I'd left, I would have spent the rest of the night wondering if you'd turned up five minutes later to a dark, empty house. Of course I'm still here.'

'Well, it's nice. Really nice.'

Nice was a useful word.

Bland.

Bren wasn't fooled by it. Her tone had said a lot more than 'nice'. Again, something swelled forcefully inside him and he reined it in, wary of how she'd react if he let it show. When an animal had been mistreated, even your kindness had to be measured in careful doses.

'Would you like to go away for a weekend some

time soon, if we can manage it?' he said instead, making it sound casual. 'Escape the pager properly?'

'Oh-h,' she breathed. 'Oh, that would be great, wouldn't it? Sydney?'

'Or the South Coast? The mountains?'

'Sydney, I think.' She sounded decisive about it, and he wondered, Because a city is more anonymous? Tougher? Safer?

'Sydney's good,' he agreed aloud. 'Boutique hotel, on the beach or the harbour, lots of good restaurants nearby. You can show me the highlights, because I really don't know the city, compared to the way I know Melbourne. Lots to do. Or we can do absolutely nothing, and no one will notice.'

She laughed. 'I'm not rostered for next weekend. Going away sounds better every second. But that's too soon.'

'Why is it too soon? I'm not rostered either, or on call. How long before that's going to happen again? There's a red-headed medical witch who does the doctors' rosters around here and she's—'

'Bribable, Bren, right now. Highly bribable. If it's really not too soon for you, let's do it next weekend.'

'Why would it be too soon for me, Nell?'

She gave a little shrug, looked vulnerable again. 'Too intense, I was thinking. Men aren't supposed to want to—and I don't want to—start living in another person's pocket as soon as they're...'

'Sleeping in each other's beds?'

'Something like that.'

'What's the story, Nell? You don't want to live in my pocket? Or you're afraid I'll be afraid you want to live in my pocket? A weekend away together isn't a pocket, in my world view.'

'No. Good. OK.'

'Leave it to me and I'll book a hotel.' He brushed the hair back from her face. 'Now, can you eat that stir-fry? Because you practically disappear when I look at you sideways, and it spooks me.'

Bren didn't stay the night.

Nell didn't ask, and he didn't offer. She felt more tired than she should have been, didn't know why, but had probably been giving off body language to that effect. When he kissed her, in a salty, aromatic haze of steam from the reheated stir-fry, his lips touched only the tiniest corner of her mouth and didn't linger there.

'Sleep well,' he whispered. 'And I'll see you Monday.'

Not tomorrow?

No, better not.

Because of the pocket thing.

Someone might become afraid that someone else might want to start living in the other person's pocket, and you couldn't have that. You could have going away together, and making love, and conversations batting back and forth like table-tennis games, full of lines that were funny and clever and even tender. But you couldn't get too close, or—

Or she'd have to stop pretending that this was a new beginning, a clean slate, as Bren had suggested it was. She'd have to remember properly, with all implications in place, that it really wasn't, that it was a continuation, that it was a half-made garment that had come unravelled and that the unravelled part would have to be knitted up again if the garment had a hope of being finished.

Deep, Nell. Too deep for this time of night.

She bolted the rest of the stir-fry down far too fast, and went to bed.

Bren plotted his choice of hotels for the coming weekend very carefully, consulted some travel guides and came up with a place on the beach front at Coogee. 'If you like the sound of it,' he told Nell on the phone on Tuesday night.

It was after nine. He'd tried her a couple of times earlier, but she hadn't been home. No prize to him for guessing where she'd been. He wondered when and what she'd eaten.

'I do like the sound of it,' she answered. 'And I've organised cover for Friday afternoon, from four o'clock on. You said you could be free by then, didn't you? It'd be great if we could get there by about ten, and have a late supper, or something.'

'We'll get in earlier than that. We're not going to drive, Nell, we're going to fly. I've booked us both on the five o'clock flight Friday evening, coming back at six on Sunday.'

'Much better. Thank you. I didn't even think of it.'

They agreed that Bren would plan Saturday, while Nell would choose her favourite Sydney places to show him on Sunday. 'Pack something dressy, and walking shoes,' he told her on Wednesday, aware that he was leaving plenty of space in their schedule in which she wouldn't require either of those things. He wondered, too, how the hotel staff would receive a request for a late check-out on Sunday morning.

On Thursday evening he packed, and hoped Nell had torn herself away from her department early enough to do the same. On Friday afternoon, it looked as if they were going to miss the plane...

'You said I should come in if I was worried,' Deanna Westway told Nell.

'Are these the first symptoms you've had?' Nell asked. It was eleven days since this patient's emergency surgery to remove her appendix, still within the window where miscarriage was possible.

The clock on the wall read ten minutes to four. She should be out of here in ten minutes and on her way to the airport, a twenty-minute drive out of town. Bren was probably in his car already, with her overnight bag as well as his own.

'Yes,' Mrs Westway answered. 'I've been taking things very cautiously since the surgery, but yesterday I did some shopping and everything seemed fine. I'm hardly sore any more. But when I woke up this morning there was some bleeding, and now I'm aching. A crampy feeling.'

'We'd better take a look, hadn't we? If you could take off your lower clothing, Mrs Westway, I'll be back in a minute.'

She slipped out, praying that no one would accost her in the corridor with urgent business. Her examination of Mrs Westway a minute or two later was reassuring for both of them. The blood loss was minor and the blood itself looked old. The cervix wasn't dilated. At the same time, the site of the surgical incision had healed well, with no sign of infection.

Nell found the baby's heartbeat, and could have sent Deanne home at that point. Instead, knowing that the mother-to-be's anxiety was very real and that miscarriage could still occur, she arranged for an ultrasound and a bed in the gynae unit overnight.

'Just to make absolutely sure,' she told Mrs Westway, and saw the relief in her eyes.

'And should I stay in bed for another few days once I'm home?'

'It certainly couldn't hurt.'

And if I don't leave now, I'll miss my flight.

Thankful that the signs were good, and that she'd been able to deal with this patient quickly, Nell grabbed her things, ran through a lightning-fast mental check-list and decided that she was free to go. OK, she'd got as far as the corridor, she could see the exit door, if she ran to her car...

'Dr Cassidy?'

She heard Margaret's voice behind her and her heart sank. She turned. And saw that the clock she could just glimpse on the far wall at the nurses' station now read four-fifteen. 'Yes, Margaret?'

'Before you go, could you—?'

'Please, Margaret, no,' she begged. 'I couldn't. Unless it's truly urgent. I'm going to Sydney for the weekend, and I'm about to miss my flight.'

Margaret looked blank, then curious, then pleased, in a motherly sort of way. 'No, it's not urgent at all. Go.' She patted Nell's shoulder. 'And have a great time.'

Was it just Nell's imagination, or did the words

'both of you' hang unspoken in the air at the end of that sentence?

She and Bren had forgotten to agree on whether they would mention the Sydney trip around the hospital. Nell hadn't intended to, and she wouldn't have if she hadn't found herself scrambling to make her flight at…sixteen minutes past four. Was that clock accurate?

After flinging a breathless 'Thanks!' back to Margaret, she ran for her car, knowing she'd be unspeakably disappointed if she was too late. There wasn't another flight to Sydney from this little airport today.

'You made it.' Bren was waiting for her by the check-in counter.

'Did I?' Nell's lungs heaved after her sprint from the long-stay parking area.

'With about thirty seconds to spare.'

'You'll have to board straight away,' the check-in clerk warned.

'I really thought I didn't have a chance.'

'Considering the way your pager co-operated for so much of last Saturday, we're doing well with miracles so far.'

Nell nodded and smiled, but felt superstitious. She considered medical miracles more reliable than personal ones. How dangerous would this weekend prove to be for her? The soaring height of her relief over making the flight and being with Bren—she felt him take her hand as they crossed the windy tarmac towards the plane—suddenly plunged into vertigo and she was scared.

CHAPTER EIGHT

THEY reached their hotel just before seven.

The streets of Coogee, fronting the arc of beach or leading down to it from the west, were crowded and noisy, but their room was quiet and private. It had its own balcony beyond louvred wooden screen doors, a granite and glass bathroom and sleek, new-looking furnishings.

'Do you want to eat out or in?' Bren asked, then held up a thick, white towelling robe he'd found hanging in one of the cupboards. His voice dropped a little, and his dark eyes held their secret smile. 'This may influence your decision.'

Nell laughed. 'Oh, you're right! One look at it, and eating in sounds like a really good idea.'

'Spicy?'

'My thoughts?' she queried, deliberately misunderstanding him. 'Yes, very!'

'Spicy food. You knew that was what I meant.'

'Guilty. Yes, I knew.'

'I noticed Thai, Indian, Vietnamese on the way in. And I smelt Italian and seafood through the taxi window, just before we turned off Coogee Bay Road.'

'Thai sounds fabulous.' She'd resisted the House of Siam three times this week. That sort of pampering could get out of hand. Instead, she'd gone for pizza on the speed dial once, and had actually cooked, sort of—eggs, or pasta with sauce from a jar—the other nights.

'Do you have strong preferences?' Bren asked. 'If you don't, you could make use of that bath while I go out and make the decisions. And you could put that robe on afterwards.'

'I'm sensing you're trying to spoil me, for some reason.'

'You can have a turn at spoiling me later, if you like. I'm not selfish.'

'No, not a bit. I'd noticed that.'

They grinned at each other, and Nell thought, this is what I want. It's all I want. We're having a hot affair. We're sneaking weekends away in gorgeous hotels. We're lounging around in fluffy, pristine robes, eating food someone else has cooked for us. We're making love whenever we choose, sleeping late, making each other laugh for no good reason. That's enough for now. If Bren tries to push it further...

She wouldn't let him.

And she hoped he wouldn't try.

Some couples kept to this sort of civilised arrangement for years, without ever feeling the need to cross certain critical boundaries. Surely she could freeze those boundaries in place without a fight.

He left a couple of minutes later, after telling her, 'I'll put in our order, then explore a bit until it's ready. Any requests?'

'Something really spicy, if you don't mind that.'

'We covered the double meaning of that word already, didn't we?'

'I'm always up for a repeat performance.'

He just raised his eyebrows at that one, and disappeared out of the door.

Nell ran the bath as soon as he'd gone, and sank into it with a sigh of bliss. Her thoughts emptied out in a way she rarely allowed—rarely could manage, in fact—and she felt drowsy and happy and hungry and expectant. Bren returned sooner than she'd anticipated, to find her still soaking beneath scented foam.

He put a plastic bag on the coffee-table, filled with what looked like way too many different dishes for just two people, while she heaved herself out of the tub. Half a minute later, he appeared in the bathroom doorway to offer, 'Let me dry you off.'

He wrapped her in a towel and then they both froze for a moment and just looked at each other.

'If you kiss me,' she told him, half a threat, half a promise, 'the food will get cold.'

'I'm aware of that. Trying to decide if I care.' He studied her mouth with eyes that had darkened from need. She could feel the length of his legs pressed against her, and the knotted muscles of his arms, holding her close.

Something jolted inside her, far too strong for comfort, and she hauled herself back from the brink with a feeling akin to vertigo. Her heart was pounding and her breath came in short jerks which she tried to control so that he wouldn't see.

'My stomach cares, I think,' she said lightly. 'Where's that robe?'

Freeing herself from his touch and slipping past him, she found it flung on the bed and slid herself into it, pulling it snugly across the front of her body and knotting the tie at her waist. Her legs were still damp and foamy from the bath, inadequately dried.

Watching him bring out dishes, silverware and stemmed glasses from the kitchenette, she said, 'Sorry, I should have thought to do that before you got back.'

'I much preferred imagining you in the bath, rather than doing this.'

'You don't have French-maid fantasies?'

'You could probably get me to have some really spectacular French-maid fantasies if you tried.'

She resisted the temptation to describe the appropriate outfit—short skirt, frilly apron, black garter belt—and said instead, in a voice that wasn't quite steady, 'Here, let me open the wine.'

He'd bought a bottle of white, already chilled. They pulled the coffee-table closer and ate on the couch, watching some televised sport that neither of them cared about. It provided a good backdrop to lazy conversation and an appreciation of the food and wine. Nell's stomach recovered from its earlier jolt and she relaxed again. Maybe what she actually wanted was a cosy affair, not a fiery one...

'So,' Bren said in a conversational tone, a few minutes later, 'when are you going to take off that robe?'

'I was, um, hoping you'd do that for me.'

'Fast or slow?'

'You choose, and I'll let you know if it's working.'

'I'm confident I can get either way to work perfectly for you, Nell.'

Hot *and* cosy. Was that possible? Wouldn't it be perfect?

* * *

They surfaced an hour or so later, glanced at the cold leftovers on the coffee-table and turned their backs.

'It's a nice night,' Bren said. 'Want to get dressed and go for a walk?'

But even the prosaic act of getting dressed took a while. Other things got in the way.

They ended up in a café, drinking cappuccinos and sharing a wedge of chocolate hazelnut torte. All around them, people were talking—serious, urban and hip. The mood was infectious, and they lingered there until after midnight. The next morning, they slept in until nine.

The weather was cooler today, with a steady wind and heavy seas. A southerly change must have come through overnight while they'd slept. Wearing jackets and walking boots, they took the ocean-front walk north to Bondi Beach, after a light breakfast, stopping several times to watch the waves foam and crash onto the rock shelf at the base of the cliffs and reading the poignant, hundred-year-old inscriptions on the headstones in Waverley Cemetery.

'Which has to occupy the most prime piece of real estate of any graveyard in the world,' Bren commented. 'Spooky at night, do you think?'

'Hard to imagine right now,' Nell said.

Big white cotton-wool clouds in the sky mimicked the Bondi Beach wind-surfers in the water, sailing fast through the blue. Sun shone on the marble and sandstone slabs, and the path that led between the graves, from Clovelly to Bondi, was dotted with morning walkers.

They didn't go all the way to Bondi's main beachfront street, but stopped at a bench seat looking north across the wide bay and watched a death-defying para-surfer skim out hundreds of metres from the shore, hoist himself on gusts of wind until he'd risen five body-lengths in the air, and rocket back towards the beach, before he turned again to head oceanwards for another run.

By the time they got back to Coogee, they were starving, and couldn't resist the smell of wood-fired pizza that lured them into an Italian eatery in the main street for a late lunch. For the first time in years, Nell drank a tall glass of sweet, fizzy cola, chunky with ice, and felt the defiant exhilaration that came with breaking good habits.

If she'd had a board and a sail and a wetsuit, she might have wind-surfed, too. Her stomach felt as if she already was.

What's happening? she wondered.

Bren thought he knew.

Hours later, he took her to dinner at an opulent harbour-front restaurant, and told her over coffee and petits fours, after a fabulous meal, 'I can't believe this, can you?'

Nell smiled. 'Which *this*, this time?'

He laughed, but insisted, 'No, I'm serious. Extremely serious, Nell.'

'Not good for you, too much of that.'

Bren ignored her. 'It's incredible that after seventeen years we could just pick up...not where we left off but in some different place that's built on knowing each other before, on having a past, and yet still feels new. Even better, too.'

'Yes...'

Was it better? Less innocent, definitely. She hadn't

known, then, about all the things there were to be frightened of.

'I like it, Nell,' he went on. 'I want more of it.'

'I got that impression…' she tried to tease, but he clearly didn't want to pull this moment back to the level they'd enjoyed for most of the time so far.

'Can we fill in the gaps?' he said. 'Push the boundaries wider? Guess that's what I'm trying to say. Or trying to ask. Just checking that I'm not wrong about this. That you feel the same.'

She gabbled, 'Bren, I'm really just looking for an affair. This is wonderful. I don't want more. I don't want…'

To have to probe the murky depths and bare my soul to you.

I don't want to join lives, because two people can't do that without far too much stripping bare.

'My priorities are different,' she finished, knowing that she'd sounded prim and cold. Terrified, too, if Bren had been listening closely enough. Had he?

Silence.

The harbour lights twinkled, reflecting in the rich dark mirror of water. At another table, laughter erupted. A waiter arrived to clear their empty plates and offer more coffee.

'Tell me about your priorities, Nell,' Bren said. His tone was hard to read.

'I—To keep things simple. This is wonderful,' she repeated. 'This weekend. But I don't want…to have you start mowing my lawn and…' she searched for something even more down beat and ordinary '…buying tissues for me when I have a cold.'

'Yeah, I'd hate that, too,' he agreed, his sarcasm

biting deep. 'Hate to see any signs of actual care from you. Wouldn't want to spend any time together when things weren't perfect.'

'Don't get angry.'

'No? I shouldn't?'

'You mentioned boundaries. I'm just telling you I'm happy to keep them where they are.'

'And what if I'm not happy about that?'

Her heart lurched.

'Then I guess you'll bail out,' she said, deliberately phrasing it as bluntly as she could.

Here was a more familiar feeling. Focus on the worst-case scenario and pretend it had already happened. Discover that you could live with it—just—and go on, with gritted teeth, from there. She'd trained herself in this for years. She preferred it, because it reduced the likelihood of disappointments.

'Are you *asking* me to bail out?'

'No. No, of course not. This is wonderful,' she said, for the third time in as many minutes. 'I'm just...' She took a breath. '...telling you that that's what you'll have to do if you're not happy with what I want.'

'You're not prepared to consider rethinking what you want?'

'No.'

'Or why you want it?'

'*This* is what I don't want!' She stood up abruptly, then sat down again and lowered her voice. 'This probing and soul-searching and analysing of each other.'

'What are you so afraid of?'

That I'll hear myself telling you about the baby.

That you won't be able to forgive me, which will remind me that I've never forgiven myself.

She understood all of this, but understanding didn't help. The little ways she'd been trying to forgive herself lately—the pizza on the speed dial, for example, and the icy glass of cola at lunch—couldn't get anywhere close enough to solving the real problem.

'You're still doing it,' she told him, the words as sharp and precise as incisions during surgery.

'I think you're wrong, Nell,' he said. He pushed back a little, leaned back in his chair. He was supposed to recognise her ice-queen tone as a very clear signal to get out of her way, but he didn't. 'You keep saying this is wonderful…'

He stopped, gave a short bark of laughter, then corrected himself. 'Well, that it *was*. Up until a minute or two ago, it was. But it's only wonderful because it's built on something that has meaning, and that has the potential to mean more.'

'I should have known you'd think that. Believe that.'

'How should you? My pure soul shines forth like a beacon, does it?'

'You spent nine years with Liz.'

'What does that have to do with anything?'

'You obviously believe—You obviously like—You're at home with all the nitty-gritty, the deep, day-to-day sharing.' She wasn't explaining this very well. 'Yes, it is about your soul,' she finally said. 'You don't have parts of it that you wouldn't bare to anyone, ever.'

'And you do?' He didn't look as if he was particularly terrified at the possibility. A little concerned, but not terrified.

'Yes. I do.'

Now, actually saying it, she'd shocked him. He hadn't expected such a blunt answer. 'I can't imagine that,' he said.

'Good. Don't try.'

'Hey, I recognise this performance.'

'It's not a performance.'

'Defence mechanism, then.'

'It's me. A big, important part of the real me, Bren. I'm sorry, I've ruined our evening. I don't know what else I could have said. I wanted to be honest. I wasn't expecting—or wanting—you to move so fast.'

'Then I'll move slower.'

'You'll move back, you mean, well out of the way.'

'I'm not bailing out, Nell.'

'Oh.'

Half of her wished he just would. Now. To get it over with.

And half of her felt such a flood of sweet relief at his statement, phrased as bluntly as she might have phrased it herself, that she discovered her hands were shaking.

'A-aren't you?' she added, almost timidly.

'No.' He was watching her hands, too, and, she suspected, interpreting them correctly. 'So are you ready to head back to our room and keep on with the wonderful part?'

'Just like that?'

'Isn't that what you want?'

Her laugh was almost a sob. '*What I want* isn't supposed to turn around and bite me on the backside.'

'I'm not sure if that's a request or a warning.'

'Bren—'

'Face it, Doctor. The ice queen has met her match.'

'Th-that's new.'

'And it could be fun.'

Even by Sunday night, when their flight touched down just after seven at Glenfallon's small airport, Bren wasn't sure if he'd weathered last night's unexpected ice storm with Nell.

On the surface he had.

Or they both had.

They'd been very good to each other today. For a woman who didn't even want a man to buy tissues for her when she had a cold, in case that was too much like a real relationship, Nell had been full of tenderness when he'd spilled boiling coffee over his hand at breakfast this morning. He'd just sat back and enjoyed her concern, wondering if she had any idea how much she was giving away. She probably thought she was only being a doctor.

They'd wangled their late check-out and spent a lazy few hours in their room—or an energetic few hours in their room, depending on your point of view. Then they'd taken a taxi to Circular Quay and a couple of ferries to nowhere in particular. It was a pleasure just to be on the harbour, taking in the sailing boats and oil tankers, the waterfront homes and the sturdy old ferry wharves with their wooden piers.

They ate lunch at a pub in the Rocks, then walked beneath the southern end of the Harbour Bridge, up to the old observatory, and back through some tourist boutiques selling opals and aboriginal art.

Another taxi ride brought them quickly to the airport, in time for a drink at one of the bars before their flight. Now they were home, and he had to decide whether to say goodbye to her in the parking area where both their cars still sat, or suggest something else. Cheese on toast and a video. Soup, buttered crumpets and sex.

Push her, or rein it in for now?

'Tired?' he asked her, as he carried their overnight bags away from the terminal.

As expected, she took the out he'd deliberately offered her. 'Yes. Nicely tired. But tired.'

They reached her car, and he put down both bags, took her in his arms, kissed her vibrant hair. 'Have a good night, then. I'll phone you during the week. Busy next weekend?'

'Caroline Archer's wedding's on Saturday. Sunday might be quiet, depending on what the department dishes up.'

'We'll try and dish up something of our own, shall we? Friday night, maybe.' He kissed her temple, her cheek, the corner of her mouth.

'Yes,' she said, more decisively than he'd expected her to. 'Let's try for Friday night.'

I-will-not-cry, I-will-not-cry, I-will-not-cry. I will *hate* myself if I cry, so I just will not do it! Nell thought.

What was it about weddings?

Biting the insides of her cheeks and watching Caroline and Declan at the altar, repeating their vows, Nell felt the scowl on her face. She must look like the Scrooge of wedding ceremonies, the one who should have turned down her invitation out of consideration for the happy couple's feelings

It was a beautiful ceremony, quietly Christian, adorned only by a couple of hymns and attended only by those closest to the bridal pair. Declan's parents in Ireland hadn't been able to come at such short notice, although they planned a visit some time next year. Two of his sisters were here, however, one with a husband and the other with a boyfriend who acted as if he fully intended to become a husband quite soon.

Caroline looked gorgeous in a simple, ankle-length gown, her lower stomach still bump-free as she'd wanted it to be when she and Nell had talked about the wedding last month. Declan had given off some panic-stricken vibes while waiting for her entrance, but as soon as she appeared, he relaxed and his face lit up, and now he spoke his words in a low, musical, utterly confident way that showed all the love he—

No.

I-will-not-cry, I-will-not-cry.

Nell bit her cheeks harder, and scowled more narrowly. She saw Emma looking her way, and studied the words to the second hymn intently. They were beautiful, and made her feel worse.

Kit and Gian had returned from their Queensland holiday just yesterday and stood in the row in front, with Bonnie between them. Nell saw them exchange a look at each other at a significant point in the ceremony, over the top of Bonnie's dark head, and that made her want to cry, too.

I *want* this. Heaven help me, I want it with Bren. I do. But it can't happen. I can't see a way through. We couldn't build something like this on top of my silence…

And talking about it was still unthinkable. Her whole body was gripped by panic, just thinking about it.

Seventeen years ago, Bren, I was pregnant with your baby. I told my mother about it. We went to Canberra, and—

I can't say it.

If I did, would he forgive me?

If he forgave me, would that help me to forgive myself?

If I could somehow do that, would we have a chance?

Where do I start?

The rest of the ceremony passed in a blur. They sang the second hymn that Nell had studied so diligently. The bridal pair disappeared to sign the register, then re-emerged to walk back down the aisle, hand in hand.

The small congregation followed them, and everyone hugged and kissed and talked. A few photographs were taken on the steps at the front, but there was another wedding scheduled here this afternoon, and early arrivals were already parking their cars and walking towards the church.

Nell examined the question she'd asked herself during the ceremony. Where did she start? Was she really contemplating that she might embark on this journey after so long? What had changed? And had it changed enough? Sometimes she thought it had, while at other times she was gripped by blind panic and just wanted to run.

*   *   *

Nell saw less of Bren than she'd expected to over the next couple of weeks. Primed to push him back to a safe distance, she instead found herself wishing she could have him closer. The accident and emergency department roster that she herself had drafted failed to co-operate, however, and they managed only a few snatched evenings.

It began to feel like the affair she'd wanted and had asked him for. He never stayed the night, never talked about plans that lay more than a few days ahead. The time they shared out of bed seemed like just a frame for the real action, rather than something to be enjoyed for itself.

She was getting exactly what she'd said she wanted, she realised, and now she didn't like it.

On a sunny October Saturday afternoon, two weeks after Caroline's wedding, she was hanging around at home, waiting for her pager to go off, when she heard a car in the driveway and looked out of her front window to find that it was Bren. Her heart lifted in its usual vertigo-inducing way, and it lifted more when he appeared in her open doorway and kissed her.

'I wasn't expecting you,' she said, having to hide her breathlessness as usual.

'I wasn't expecting you to be here,' he answered. 'Just dropped in on the off-chance.'

'Quiet day in the department, apparently. I haven't been called in.'

'I've been looking at houses all day.'

'So you're on your way home?'

'Sort of.'

Did that mean he wasn't sure he'd get there any time soon?

'How's it going?' she asked quickly. 'The house hunt, I mean. I thought you had an agent scouting out places for you.'

'Yes, but no one's selling on Grafton Street, despite the guy's best efforts to talk up the idea to various empty-nesters, and it's time to get something settled, so I'm looking more widely now.'

'Did you find anything?'

'Couple of places. One that doesn't need a thing done to it, and another one I like much better that needs heaps of work. If I could just mix and match…'

'Do you want to do the work?'

'Not particularly. But the place is sort of calling to me, and I have a horrible feeling I'm going to make an offer on it this week.'

He didn't ask for her opinion, or mention taking her to see the two houses, and she had that feeling, again, that she was getting exactly what she'd asked for in this relationship and was perversely discovering that she didn't want it after all.

'Want some tea? Coffee? Beer?' she asked him.

'What I'd really like is permission to sit in that cane chair on your front veranda and experiment with something.' He gave his beguiling grin—not the secret smile that she loved, but the big, open, warm grin-thing that she loved just as much.

'Well, of course you can sit there!' she said.

Experiment? What did he mean by that?

'But I'll take coffee as well. Let me just duck out to the car for a sec first.'

'I'll put on a pot.'

She went back to the kitchen and set up her drip filter coffee-maker, laughing cynically at herself. Make it a really, really good cup of coffee, Nell, in a really big mug, and see if that makes him stay longer—for a second cup, a beer, dinner, or even the whole night. Find some biscuits to go with it, and check that they're not stale. Put a bottle of wine in the fridge, just in case.

The coffee was just starting to drip into the glass jug, as dark as Bren's eyes, when she heard the lilt of music coming down the hall. What was that? Not her compact disc player, or someone's car radio. Why did it sound so close?

She almost tiptoed to the open front door and saw Bren sitting in a lazy slouch in one of the two cane chairs on her veranda, with a shaft of afternoon sun sneaking under its western end and bathing him in light from the chest down. He had an ankle crossed over the opposite knee, and an acoustic guitar on his lap, and he was playing.

Singing, too.

She stopped, silent, and listened to him, hoping he wouldn't realise she was there. What was this? After a few more bars she recognised an old heavy metal classic, but Bren wasn't playing it that way, he was playing it like a folk song, drawing out a thoughtful, emotional meaning to the driving lyrics that could have made you laugh at the incongruity or cry at the unexpected poignancy.

At this time of year, the citrus groves that surrounded Glenfallon were all in blossom, and the mild air smelled astonishingly sweet. Half the time, the locals forgot to notice it. Some people even claimed they got sick of it. Nell didn't, but she did forget about it for days at a time.

Today, listening to Bren, and watching the unself–conscious pleasure he got from playing, she breathed it in with all its aching symbolism and knew, once and for all, that she loved Bren, and that she wanted him sitting on her front veranda with his guitar for the rest of her life. She knew exactly what it would take from her—she'd known for weeks—but only now did she believe she might actually do it.

She kept watching him—the angle of his neck and shoulder, the dark shape of his head, the way his chest moved when he breathed and the way he lifted his head when he reached a longer, higher note. And she must have sighed, or shifted her weight and made the wooden door threshold creak, because he got to the end of the chorus and turned to her.

'See, this is what I want,' he said. 'A veranda like this, where I can sit and do this. I've given up on the veggie garden and the pottery.'

'Were you ever serious about those?' She came towards him, trying to smile and keep it light.

'Nope. This, though, I want. I knew I did, and now that I've tried it out at your place…'

'Which house has the veranda?'

'The one that needs the work. A new kitchen, a new bathroom, a bad addition knocked off and replaced. New wiring, probably. It's two streets over. It faces south, like this place, with the main bedroom, the second bedroom and the back garden getting all the northern sun.'

'Close,' she said, trying not to make that sound important.

'Convenient,' he agreed. 'There's a lot to be said for geographical compatibility in an affair.'

Move closer. Live here. Forget the affair. I love you, Bren. All we need to do is…

Talk to each other. But I'm still not brave enough for that. Not today. Let me work up to it. You'll have things to forgive. I'm not sure that you will forgive them. And I have other people to talk to first.

'Coffee's probably ready,' she said, and turned back into the house before she showed too much of what she felt.

Nell opened the door in response to Bren's knock on Tuesday night wearing the pink cotton top she'd worn to her father's, khaki pants and the look of a woman in love.

Bren knew the look because he'd seen its betraying flame of white light on Liz's face when she'd first told him about Simon, and it hit him like the unexpected turns and dips of a roller-coaster ride.

'Come in,' she said, sounding breathless. 'I'm cooking.'

She hovered in the doorway, unconsciously expectant. Did she know how much she looked as if she was waiting for his kiss? Her brilliant blue eyes were wide and bright and naked, and her mouth was soft.

Bren stepped forward and cradled her jaw in his hand. 'Smells wonderful.'

'It's la—'

But the word got lost on his lips. He didn't care what she was making. It smelled wonderful, and so did she, and at the moment she was way more important. He wrapped his arms around her, and heard the soft sounds she made—sounds of delight and appreciation, which she didn't try to hide.

He kissed her more deeply, and cupped his hands across her bottom, just where it folded into a crease at the top of each thigh.

I could take her to bed right now, he thought. The way I did Saturday afternoon, before we even finished our coffee. She wouldn't be able to string two words together. If the dinner burned, neither of us would care.

Something made him curb his impatience, however. He wanted to see more of that love light on Nell's face, make sure he hadn't got it all wrong, because in so many ways it just didn't make sense.

If Nell felt so strongly—and, lord, he hoped she did!—then why was she still holding back so much?

Oh, not right now.

She pressed herself against him with as much need and pleasure as any man could want. He hardened against her lower stomach and she only pressed closer. She whispered his name, raked her nails softly against his neck and inside the collar of his shirt, down to his shoulder, letting their crescents bite just enough to send pulses of electricity shooting all the way through him.

She definitely wasn't holding back now.

But at other times, yes, her doing so was painfully apparent. He remembered her hard-edged talk of 'just an affair' at the harbour-front restaurant three and a half weeks ago, and the look of panic he still saw in her face sometimes, telegraphed every bit as clearly as the love he thought he saw tonight.

He kept trying to signal to her that panic wasn't

necessary. That was partly why he'd made a point of coming over after his house-hunting expedition on Saturday. He'd wanted to sit there with his guitar, yes, and try to work out whether the right veranda was really worth the new bathroom and kitchen, and the other major work that his favourite house needed.

But he hadn't been joking about geographical compatibility. He'd wanted Nell to realise that he was putting together the same self-sufficient existence she apparently had no desire to change for herself.

Maybe the strategy had worked. Maybe this was why she seemed less wary and more giving tonight.

He pulled back, painting a final brushstroke on her mouth with his lips, then coming back for just one more taste. 'Now you can tell me what you're cooking.'

'Lasagne.' She wrapped her arms around her body, and Bren couldn't tell if it was a gesture of defence or of need. 'I'll take one dish of it out to Dad's on Sunday, and we'll eat the other one tonight, now, fresh out of the oven. There's salad, and I've opened some wine.'

'Mmm, when you asked me if I wanted to drop around for dinner, I didn't expect something as good as this.'

She shrugged, and blushed—unless that was the heat from the oven, or the heat from their kiss. 'I got home early enough, since we had a quiet department today, and I felt like cooking. I'm glad you were free.'

'Sitting by the phone,' he answered, mocking himself.

He hadn't been, but when it had rung and he'd

heard her voice, he'd had a hard time not jumping into his car the moment he'd put it down.

'Hungry, I hope.'

He followed her into the kitchen and she grabbed two oven mitts, opened the oven door and slid out an enormous pan of bubbling lasagne. 'I could put a fair bit of that away, yes,' he answered.

The open bottle of wine sat on her countertop next to two stemmed glasses, and they both reached for it at the same time, bumping hands and almost knocking the bottle over. They laughed, and he grabbed her fingers, and suddenly they were kissing again, all over each other, elated and happy and filled with their secret.

He touched her hair and her breasts and those delicious thigh creases again, his whole body tingling and crying its need. He only managed to hold back from carrying her to the bedroom by promising himself that it would be even better later on. They already had each other on a hair trigger. Delaying the inevitable explosion would make it even more intense.

Nell had music playing. He'd barely heard it until now, but suddenly the female singer's voice rose in volume, smoky and intense, echoing the surge in his own feelings, and he found himself thinking, It was never like this with Liz. How could I have been wrong about that for so long?

They lingered over their meal for nearly an hour, talking about politics and ecology and travel. Nell's opinions showed their usual bite and wit and cleverness, and Bren found himself laughing, egging her on, enjoying her sharp mind and the sense that they were each keeping the other one on their toes.

When a silence finally fell, and their plates were empty, their wineglasses down to the dregs and their stomachs replete, Nell said softly, 'Can we go to bed now, Bren?'

So they did that, and he was glad he'd waited for her to make the move. Nell explored every inch of his body with her lips, letting her hands brush and fall where they wanted to, tantalising him, making that hair trigger tremble. He let her know exactly how powerful this was for him, didn't try to suppress his body's shuddering or its cries.

Her own climax seemed quieter and more private, and when they lay together quietly afterwards, she leaned up on her elbow and reached across his chest, ruffling her fingers through the hair that grew there, touching him absently, as if she wasn't really thinking about it any more. He got the impression that she wanted to speak, to tell him something, or ask him something.

'Spit it out,' he said.

But she shook her head, stayed there with her breasts spilling against him, frowning.

Holding back again, he recognised, in yet another way. Not hard-edged, not fearful, but thoughtful, as if examining what she felt from a new and more critical angle.

A minute later, she gave a sigh, then answered, 'No, I sort of knew this already... I don't think you're the one I need to spit it out to.'

'So who is?'

She smiled, because she knew she was supposed to. 'I'll get back to you on that one.'

Bren didn't try to get anything more out of her that

night, but felt edgy about it. If this was a race, he was still a long way from crossing the finish. They'd had such a great talk over dinner, and only now did he consider the fact that none of it had been personal.

He wondered if that meant something. He hadn't been steering the conversation, and he didn't think that Nell had either, but he wondered all the same.

He stayed all night, and Nell didn't throw out any vibes that she wanted him to go away. In the morning, they both woke early and had time for a brisk walk, a shared shower and a quick breakfast, and left for the hospital within a minute of each other.

Later that day, he phoned to tell his real estate agent to make an offer on the house he loved, not the house that was sensible.

CHAPTER NINE

NELL heard the ambulance siren before she'd even pressed the button on her key fob to lock her car. The vehicle turned into the driveway as she quickened her pace towards the hospital's rear entrance, and braked to a stop in the emergency bay, out of sight, as she pushed open the door. Bren was just turning into the parking area behind her.

At the nurses' station, she met Margaret, who told her, 'We've just got a new admission. Patient in severe pain, with falling blood pressure and a rigid abdomen. That's the information relayed from the ambulance. He looks terrible, and can hardly speak. You must have heard him coming in.'

'If that was the ambulance that brought him just now, then, yes. What more information do we have? Anything?'

'It's the mayor, God bless him, Geoff Peacock. Fifty-three years old, and I know he's had a few health problems in the past. Wife is following in a taxi. She was too distraught to drive, and not ready to go in the ambulance.'

'Find someone to look after her as soon as she gets here—she's on the hospital board. Better yet, do it yourself, Margaret, if you remotely have time.'

'Because she's on the hospital board?' Margaret threw out a sceptical, sidelong glance.

Nell glared back. 'Don't look at me like that,

148

Margaret. I'm going to be realistic, not brimming with egalitarian principles. And cynicism aside, it's not just the board thing. Any wife in this situation needs our best care. From memory, yes, you're right, Geoff Peacock's not in great shape physically. If it is a ruptured aortic aneurism…'

A quick examination, with assistance from Helen Bartram, confirmed what the ambulance officers had reported. Geoff Peacock was in terrible pain. He was pale and sweaty, and could only just manage to gasp out answers to Nell's questions.

The pain came from just below his diaphragm, and seemed to go all the way through to his spine. His blood pressure was still falling, and his abdomen felt as tight as a drum.

As she'd done with Zach Lloyd some weeks ago, Nell didn't wait until she'd refined her diagnosis. The symptoms pointed to internal bleeding, so she ordered a rapid infusion of fluids and called for Bren. If this was a ruptured aneurism or duodenal ulcer, they could lose this patient very quickly.

'Mrs Peacock's here.' Margaret appeared with the news. 'I've talked to her briefly, but she's anxious and upset and she wants to see you.'

'I'm sending him for surgery, Margaret. I'm not waiting on this. I've already got theatre staff preparing, and Bren's postponed his scheduled list. Oh, here he is.'

Her heart lifted, and she had to fight to keep her face in its usual serious mask.

Here was Andy Fairbrother, too, ready to wheel Mr Peacock along to the operating suite. 'Not yet,' Nell told him. 'Don't go anywhere.'

The first fluid bag was almost through, so she put up another one. 'Almost there, Mr Peacock, it won't be long now.'

He nodded, still grey-faced and unable to speak. He closed his eyes.

'I'll tell his wife about the surgery,' Margaret said quietly. 'You'll want to see her, though, won't you?'

'Definitely. Send her in. Meanwhile, Bren, we need to talk.' Nell turned quickly to him. They walked away from the bedside together and she spoke quietly. 'The history isn't encouraging. He's a smoker, not in good shape. I'm pouring in fluids, but there's a real chance you'll lose him, Bren.'

'Have we got blood on hand?'

'Yes, already ordered. Fortunately, we already had the right information from a previous operation.' She sketched the relevant history as quickly as she could, and watched the way Bren absorbed it.

'Clive's on anaesthesia this morning, and he's good,' he said. 'Leave it to me, Nell. You've worked fast, and that's a big help. You'll have to tell Mrs Peacock, though. She'll want to talk to him, and it might be goodbye. She needs to be told.'

'I know. I'll make sure it's clear.'

Lord, Bren knew how much she hated doing this, but he was right. There was no choice today. She couldn't delegate this to Margaret or Helen, and Bren himself didn't have time.

She felt his hand against her back, making a light caress that ended with a stroke of his fingers on the back of her neck. He bent close, almost close enough to kiss her, and his forehead brushed hers softly. The moment was over almost before it had begun.

Then they both heard a movement and there was Janelle Peacock, with Margaret hovering in the background. Both women must have seen the way Bren had touched her and the look in his eyes.

Janelle Peacock narrowed hers, while Margaret tactfully disappeared. The mayor's wife was red-faced and shaking, holding tears back with difficulty. 'What on earth is this?' she hissed. Nell recognised her desperation and her fear.

'Where my husband's welfare is concerned, I have to warn you, *nothing* gets in my way,' Mrs Peacock continued. Her chest heaved and her hands were shaking. 'Geoff is too important to this town. I've heard the rumours about you two, and this consultation had better be professional to the utmost degree or you will hear about it, I promise you!'

'Rumours?' Nell heard Bren mutter under his breath. She could see the sudden tension in his shoulders. 'Hell, already?'

She herself chose not to respond to Mrs Peacock's heavy-handed threat in any way.

'Your husband is going into surgery immediately, Mrs Peacock,' she said instead, as Bren vanished down the corridor, on his way to scrub for the operation.

'Oh, I knew it. I knew it was serious.'

'We suspect there's been some kind of rupture, possibly an aortic aneurism. Signs are that he's bleeding internally, and we can't let that go. I have to tell you that there's some risk, however.'

'Risk?'

'That the blood loss will have been too severe, and he won't come through the operation. I know that's hard news, and there's just no way to soften it. There's no time either. We want him in surgery as soon as possible.'

'Can I—?'

'Yes, you can see him. Please, see him, and talk to him, think about what you want to say.'

In case it's your last chance.

She didn't spell that out, but saw that Mrs Peacock understood.

'You can stay with him until he's ready to go in, Mrs Peacock,' she said. 'The surgical staff will still need a few minutes to prepare. Come with me now.'

She took Janelle by the shoulders and pivoted her in the right direction. The woman was rigid. Still smarting from the desperate dig about 'rumours', Nell nonetheless felt as if she understood, and found her easier to handle, in many ways, than Zach Lloyd's mother had been a few weeks ago. Bren had had more trouble.

The lady mayoress wasn't the type that crumpled and looked for sympathy. She was the type that lashed out, blustered her way through her fear, and she'd probably been very honest just now. Where her husband's welfare was concerned, nothing would get in her way, and she'd use whatever weapons came to hand.

'Including the fact that Bren and I went for a walk together at six-fifteen this morning, along her brother-in-law's street,' Nell muttered under her breath.

She knew Neil Peacock slightly. He owned a local farm machinery business, and shared a back fence with her neighbour three doors down.

'Here he is, Mrs Peacock,' she said.

'Oh, Geoff. Oh, Geoff, can you talk to me? Can you hear me?'

The mayor's eyes were closed, surrounded by pallid skin that glistened with sweat. He didn't open them and he didn't reply, but he nodded and managed a faint smile for his wife.

'I love you, darling. Be strong for me, won't you? Please? And I'll see you when the operation's over. I know I will…'

Nell was busy elsewhere, juggling several patients at once, when Geoff's surgery was completed. Bren managed to get through to her after surgery on the first patient on his scheduled list. 'Touch and go, and we needed the blood, but we sent him up to the ICU in better shape than I'd feared.'

Nell wondered about Janelle's response to this. Bren would have found her and told her. She might have slumped, cried or remained as rigid as she'd been before, lashing out so that she didn't simply collapse.

She didn't see Bren again until lunch—she was eating a sandwich in her office—when he ducked into the department to give her a more detailed report.

'How was his wife?' She finished her sandwich and wiped her mouth on the paper napkin provided with it.

'Still making threats,' Bren answered.

'I wondered.'

'Not surprised?'

'Not really. She could have gone either way, I thought.'

'You have more sympathy for that type than for the crumblers, don't you?' He sat down on the corner of her desk. They hadn't kissed or touched. Maybe the 'rumours' Janelle Peacock had mentioned were still getting in the way.

'Since most people prefer the crumblers, I don't think that's a bad thing,' Nell said.

'You're a study in contradictions, Nell.'

'No, I'm not! I think I'm pretty consistent.'

He laughed. 'I like contradictions. Let me think it, even if it's not true. What do you think about the substance of what she said, though?'

'What do I think of the fact that there are rumours? That people have guessed?'

'Well, that she suspected us of inappropriate professional behaviour.'

'I—That's—I—'

Oh, he was right! She *was* a mass of contradictions!

She hadn't really thought about Janelle Peacock's words from that angle. She'd been thinking as a doctor. What did the woman's trembling threats say about how she was handling her husband's emergency hospitalisation? And if Glenfallon's mayor survived his surgery, how long before he could be pronounced out of danger?

But when she looked at it from a different perspective, problems that she hadn't considered until now poured into her lap like a flood of spilled drink. The rumours would spread. People would love that word 'unprofessional' and they'd love the suggestion of a hot, secret affair. Half the town would know, and every single member of the hospital staff from the chairman of the board to the part-time weekend cleaners.

Which wouldn't matter, perhaps, if she could see

her way clearly ahead to a rosy future, containing a respectable public commitment between herself and Bren.

But she couldn't.

Last night had been wonderful, as always. Better, because she was trying harder to make the right connection within the boundaries they'd set.

Bren had been looking seriously at houses on the weekend. She had to be logical about that, and accept that it was a good thing. Every time she told herself this was just an affair, and she didn't have to think about the future, didn't have to define her feelings any further, she had a blissful, perfect time. But every time she thought about the next step, she panicked.

She'd already decided to ask for a week of the leave that was owing to her—she always had leave owing, which probably said a lot about her life—so that she could fly to Queensland to see her mother.

The sooner the better.

But would it solve anything, if they confronted each other, or would it only make her feelings worse?

At some point, the real confrontation would have to happen between her and Bren. She knew it, and yet she had no real confidence that talking was a cure. If she had believed that, she would have talked about it long ago. To Dad, perhaps, or to her friends, if not to Mum.

She felt stuck, and scared.

Again.

Still.

Ground she thought she'd gained was suddenly gone again.

'Don't look so frightened,' Bren told her softly, and

her vision focused. 'We can withstand the gossip, can't we?'

He bent towards her and slid off her desk. His arms came around her, but she fended them off, ignoring the terrifying charge of need that bolted through her. 'No, Bren, not now. If someone came in…'

'You were caught dancing in my arms a few weeks ago, and the world didn't end.'

Yes, it did, she wanted to say. My safe little world, so carefully built up and so well protected, *did* end that night.

She didn't say it, of course, just dammed the words back behind their concrete wall as usual. When she did speak, her voice was as crisp as burned toast. 'I'm the head of this department, with responsibilities all over the hospital. It would hardly look good if I was discovered—'

'Kissing the man you love, Nell?' he finished for her softly.

Love?

Yes, she did love him. She already knew that. He'd found his way into her soul seventeen years ago, and somehow, through all she'd lived through since, he'd never left. She loved him as if love were an organ in her body, working in tandem with her lungs and her stomach and her heart.

That didn't solve anything.

It just scared her more.

'It would look great,' he went on, smiling at her and trying to get her to smile back. 'Extremely cute, and politically a winner. Word would go out. She's human. She has a beating heart. People might even take down some of the notices.'

'The notices?'

'The "all staff must" notices.'

'Those are necessary.' She felt the tightening of her own mouth. It was miles from kissable, and she was glad of that. 'They're up for a reason, Bren. I don't simply invent them to—'

'Hey, I'm teasing. I know they're up for a reason. I know they're part of your strategy. You run a good department. You have a management style that not everyone would choose, but it gets results and you're respected for that. I'm thinking that if everyone knew that Dr Cassidy was in love with the new general surgeon, you might earn something softer and stronger than respect as well.'

Nell closed her eyes.

So he knew how she felt, and he was prepared to say it out loud.

Fabulous.

Should she lie outright and deny it? Ignore it? Admit it?

And could he possibly be telling her, *now* of all times, *here* of all places, that he felt the same? He could be as inconsistent as she was.

'Bren…' she said helplessly, eyes still closed.

She felt his hand on her hair, stroking it, running his fingers down to her neck. He'd have it loose in another minute, and she couldn't care. She felt his cheek rub warm across hers, and a tiny bump from his nose. She lifted her face, eyes still tight shut, pretending this wasn't happening. Not here. Not now. He touched her mouth, first with the ball of his thumb, then with his lips.

Hers parted at once, trembling with their usual eagerness to taste him. She melted inside. How could they do this to each other? It was too powerful, and not safe. Especially not here, in her office, in the middle of her professional domain.

Too late, she heard footsteps, a perfunctory knock and then the click of her door. 'Dr Cassidy, could you...?' The voice stopped.

Nell flinched as if she'd touched an electrified fence, opened her eyes and sat back hard in her chair, jolting her spine.

It was Margaret, thank goodness, not Andy Fairbrother, or short-tempered Nissa Thomas, one of the nurses whom Nell had had to yell at more than once.

But Margaret was hiding a smile.

I don't want her smiling, Nell thought. She's already putting this together with the fact that we went to Sydney for a weekend. I don't want her thinking she can tell everyone about this because it's good news. It's not.

'I'd appreciate it if you'd wait for more than a quarter of a second, Margaret, between knocking and opening the door,' she said in her most glacial tone. 'You might as well omit the knock altogether if you don't.'

She didn't care how she sounded, she just wanted to get the message across. In this department, it was always about results, not about feelings, and that applied whether the issue at hand was saving lives or down playing the fact that someone had caught you kissing a surgeon at your office desk.

'Right,' Margaret answered. 'I wanted to see if you were free to look at a patient.'

'I will be. I have something to resolve with Dr Forsythe first.'

Her hard stare dared Margaret to mention this to a living soul. She felt a little twinge of remorse about it. She and Margaret had been getting on well lately, and the older nurse was wonderfully competent and even-tempered.

It couldn't be helped, she decided.

Margaret ducked out again, closing the door carefully.

'We'd better not "resolve" for too long,' Bren said, teasing her.

She glared at him, the way she'd glared at poor Margaret. 'We'll talk later.'

'Hmm, a few interesting issues have come up, haven't they?'

'This is just what I didn't want. Did you make an offer on that house, by the way?'

'Yes, but it wasn't high enough, apparently, and the sellers knocked it back.'

'Make another one. You don't want things dragging on.'

'Is there a personal resonance to that statement?'

'No!'

He just laughed at that, making her usual weapons of distance and coldness wilt like cartoon guns that shot daisies instead of bullets. 'Go and see your patient, Nell,' he said.

She went out to her father's that night on an impulse, bearing the lasagne she'd made yesterday as if this was the reason for her visit, although she'd intended to freeze it until one of her more usual trips on the weekend. At the hospital, which she hadn't torn herself away from until nearly eight, Geoff Peacock remained in a serious but stable condition after his surgery.

Since she'd phoned ahead to check that her father was home, he had the outside lights on and was expecting her. 'Shame I've already eaten,' he said, eyeing the big dish in her hands. 'Have you, though?'

'Not yet, but don't waste this on me. I had a pan of it last night. Toast is fine.'

Dad didn't say anything, just pulled out a chair for her at the kitchen table and put today's newspaper down in front of her. That would have been a welcome gesture normally, but tonight she wanted to talk. Trying to gather her thoughts and form them into words, she barely noticed him digging around in the freezer and putting something on the stove to heat up.

'Cup of tea?' he said.

She nodded. 'As long as you're having one.'

'I will, since you're here.'

They smiled at each other. 'Let's get it straight, Dad,' she said. 'Do you actually want one, or are you just keeping me company?'

'Keeping you company is a good enough reason to want one, don't you think? Hate it when people drop in and I offer them a beer or a cuppa and they knock it back. It's about communication, not thirst.'

She laughed. 'You're right...' She cleared her throat. 'And I want to communicate a bit tonight.'

'Yeah?'

'I wanted to ask—You've never said—You never said much, seventeen years ago, when Mum talked me into...' Just say it! 'Terminating the pregnancy.'

Chair legs scraped the floor as Dad sat down. He'd

put the electric kettle on, but it hadn't even yet begun to sing. He was right about the lubricating effect of shared tea. She should have waited. She was doing this all wrong, and he'd—

'Oh, good lord, Eleanor! Is that still on your mind?' He didn't wait for her to answer. 'Because Bren's come back?' Again, he didn't wait. 'Does he know?'

'No, he doesn't know. But, yes, it's on my mind, because I'm going to have to tell him.'

Dad didn't seem fazed by this reasoning, which suggested that he understood what lay behind it.

'Mmm, I suppose you are,' he said, after some thought. 'You think he'll blame you, even though, in the end, you never actually had to go through—'

'Why shouldn't he blame me, when I blame myself?' she cut in heatedly. 'I want to know what you think, Dad.'

'Oh, Nell...!' he groaned.

'Do you think Mum was right? You stood in the background. I can see now, obviously, that the two of you weren't communicating very well by that stage. You told me at the time that she was right, but I wonder how much of that was because you didn't want to rock the boat.'

'Do you think if you'd known I was on side, you would have stood up to her, is that it?'

'*Were* you on side?'

He made a noncommittal sound, but he didn't speak.

For the first time, Nell understood a little of what her mother had found maddening and impossible in him—that he stepped back from conflict and sometimes from responsibility. He slavishly mended fences at times when he needed to take a stand. The understanding didn't dampen her love for him, and it helped in a strange way.

Life was complex. Marriage was. People were. It was…good to discover that Mum was in the right in some areas. She wasn't the villain in this. Not really. She'd had the right intentions. Maybe there wasn't a villain.

Nell felt the sharp prick of tears.

'Go on, Dad,' she whispered, through a tightened throat. 'I need to know. I need to hear from you on this.'

'I thought you should have made your own decision,' he said at last. 'I was waiting for you to fight. You're a fighter by nature.'

'Would you have stepped in then? Supported me?'

'Whatever you'd decided, your mother would have had plans for it. How to raise the baby. How to deal with the loss if you'd had it adopted.'

'What happened, in the end, was probably the one thing she didn't have a plan for,' Nell said.

'No,' her father agreed. 'I don't think she was kind to you about that.'

'No? You don't?'

'Acting as if it made the whole thing disappear. It never really did, did it? That's why we're talking about it now. And me… I tried to be kind. In my way. Wasn't enough, probably.'

'You could have been stronger.'

He was silent again, his head fallen forward a little, as if admitting to his failure. 'Would it have helped you now, though?' He looked up again. 'What's the problem now?'

The electric kettle boiled and clicked off, but they both ignored it.

'The problem now…' Nell struggled again '…is that I can't forgive myself, even after all this time, and I don't know why.'

'Sounds as if it needs some more thought. You were planning to go up and see your mother soon. Is that still on?'

'Yes, I've put in a leave application, and approached a couple of doctors about cover. I'm hoping to head up there at the end of next week.'

'What will you say?' He got up and began to make the tea, as well as stirring the pot on the stove. Something inside it had begun to smell good and familiar. 'Don't hurt her, love,' he said. 'She wanted the best for you, that's all. Problem is, she's often convinced that she's the only one who knows what the best is, and how to get it. The one time that I came up with a plan for the two of us, it didn't work out.'

'When was that, Dad?'

'When I convinced her to marry me, and that we could be happy together, the three of us.'

'She didn't want to? I always assumed it was her idea.' Nell had known her mother had already been pregnant, but had never asked about the alternatives she and Dad might have considered. 'You know,' she went on, 'bossy and practical.' She made a rough mimicry of her mother's tone. 'We're having a baby, we'll get married, we'll do it right.'

'No, that was me, saying that. She would have—'

'Dear God, terminated the pregnancy, too?'

'No, but she'd already put together a list of homes for pregnant girls. She was going to research them,

find the best, book herself in, have the baby—you—
and give you away. But I persuaded her. I painted this
rosy picture, told her I loved her. I think that's why
she wanted you to have the termination. To take away
Bren's best argument—that you were having a baby
together. She was so ambitious for you.'

'Bren never knew. We had our big fight before I'd
begun to take the signs seriously.'

'Talk to her about it, Nell.'

'I'm going to.'

'And talk to him.'

'Yes.' Her heart lurched in her chest, just thinking
about it.

Dad ladled something into a big, deep bowl, which
turned out to be his home-made pea and ham soup. It
zapped her straight back to winter Saturday nights as
a child when he'd make it, and bake potatoes in foil
in an open fire.

He was more domesticated than her mother in many
ways, and a more natural nurturer. Perhaps Mum
should have worked, and he should have stayed at
home, but that sort of role reversal was still a rare
thing, even now. Nell wasn't convinced it would have
been enough to keep her parents together. Their problems and their differences had run deeper.

Dad sat at the table again and pulled the newspaper
towards him, after lifting off the top section for Nell
to read. He seemed to feel that they'd said everything
now, and maybe he was right.

Nell left for Queensland the following Saturday morning, having worked heavy hours for the rest of the
week. She'd seen very little of Bren, although he'd

kept her updated on Geoff Peacock, who was slowly improving. There had been no further threats from his wife.

Nell had only mentioned her trip to Bren in passing, and he'd apparently taken it at face value. She was going for a holiday with her mother, and she'd worked extra hours in advance of her time off to make it easier on the doctors who were taking over her load while she was gone.

Mum met her at the airport, looking her usual well-groomed self in a dark business suit, with her strawberry blonde hair freshly coloured and styled. They went home to a two-bedroom unit in a high-rise building that was only a few years old. It overlooked the Brisbane River, just downstream of the city centre, perfectly placed for urban work and leisure.

As soon as Nell had put her suitcase and carry-on bag in the spare bedroom-cum-study, Mum asked proudly, 'So what do you think? Better than the other place, isn't it?'

'It's lovely,' Nell answered sincerely.

She could see that the new place had just the right ingredients to make her mother happy—a sophisticated location, pristine decor and appliances that were easy to keep clean. The place was filled with items that showed a woman who revelled in living alone and catering only to her own tastes and needs.

There were a couple of photos of Nell herself, and even one that included both her parents, but most showed her mother at professional gatherings, or enjoying herself with groups of women friends.

'Now, while you're here,' Mum said. 'I have concert tickets, and theatre tickets, and there are a couple of new restaurants we can try.'

They had a busy week, and Nell realised that it would be all too easy to let the time slip away and never bring up the deeply personal issues she wanted to discuss. If she'd been prepared to ignore those issues, she would have enjoyed herself very much. As things stood, however, they hung over her at times.

Mum had designated Thursday evening as 'a quiet night at home', which promised to offer the opportunity Nell needed. They had an elegantly set out picnic-style meal of gourmet deli treats—smoked salmon, Tasmanian cheese, prepared salads and long sticks of bread, as well as white wine.

'Do you have the number for the nearest pizza restaurant on your telephone speed dial, Mum?' Nell asked her while they ate.

As expected, she received a look of horrified astonishment in reply. 'No! Why? Do you?'

'I'm considering it. A couple of my friends seem to find it convenient, and I'd been wondering if it was a universal thing, and I was just hopelessly un-cool.'

'I don't even like pizza much.'

'No... OK, forget it, then.' She wasn't sure why she'd tried to tease Mum. Hardly surprising that it hadn't worked. Mum wasn't Bren.

It took Nell longer to work around to the more important areas, but she got to them in time for coffee and chocolates. Again, Mum seemed astonished and verging on horrified at the fact that she'd brought any of it up.

'You can't possibly regret what you couldn't control, Nell,' she said. 'You had the best possible out-

come that day, and I told you that at the time. I was
intensely relieved.'

'Were you?'

'Yes, of course! I'd been so worried, and so afraid
for you. Don't think I took any of it lightly, Nell, or
that the advice I gave you was ill-thought-out. You
were too bewildered and shocked to know what you
were feeling at the time, but you must feel it in hindsight, surely? The same relief that I felt then?'

'No. I don't. Maybe I should. But I…haven't been
able to. Even after so long. I'm not sure why.'

'And Bren Forsythe is back in Glenfallon, and that's
freshened it all for you again. I'm glad his health is
so good now. Again, though, knowing that it might
not have been, his going off to Melbourne in a pet was
the best thing that could have happened.'

'In a *pet*?'

'In a huff. In a rage. Whatever you'd call it. You
were too *young*, Nell!' She opened her hands, then
flattened them on the table, making the surface of
Nell's coffee jitter for a second or two. 'That was the
thing I kept coming back to. And don't tell me I can't
know that, because I can! I was far too young myself
when I got married and had you, only a few months
older than you'd have been.'

'Dad told me last week that he'd talked you into it.
I never realised that.'

To Nell's surprise, Mum smiled as she remembered.

'He was pretty hard to argue against that day,' she
said. 'I wish he could have been like that more often.
We both misunderstood who each other was, back
then. Because we were too *young*, Nell. It always

comes back to that. Please, don't pickle yourself in regret...'

'Or anger?'

'Or anger. I won't accept that you have any reason to be angry with me, in particular. I stand by what I thought then.'

I wish I could, Nell thought, but she didn't say it aloud. Certainty. That was one of the crucial things that was missing, she realised, and she respected it in her mother now a little better than she had before.

She flew back to Glenfallon on Saturday afternoon, feeling that she'd grown a little closer to Mum, and that she had a better understanding of Mum's priorities and choices, even if she still couldn't fully agree with them.

CHAPTER TEN

NELL hauled her own suitcase out of the back of the taxi, since the driver didn't seem inclined to help.

Possibly he was annoyed with her for changing her mind, three times, as to where she wanted him to take her. Climbing in at Glenfallon airport, she'd first told him the hospital, then her home address, then Bren's place, then the hospital again.

It was likely that she'd have to order another taxi, in half an hour or so, to take her home, and she hoped a different one would show up next time. It must be around three o'clock. Didn't taxi drivers change shifts about now? Many of this hospital's nurses did.

Nell felt way too keyed up about the possibility of seeing Bren. Unable to remember the roster she'd drawn up a few weeks ago, she wasn't sure if he'd be here or not, but if he wasn't, she could pretend she was here purely to check up on her department. The rest of the staff would find this only too plausible.

'Nell? Nell, that's you, isn't it?'

She heard a voice calling her name as she walked towards the main entrance, but it definitely wasn't Bren. She turned and saw Kit Di Luzio, née McConnell, coming towards her.

'Hi,' she said, and they gave each other a hug.

'Where have you got back from?' Kit had seen the suitcase. Hard to miss.

'Brisbane. I had a week with my mother.'

'You look good, Nell.'

'Thanks.' She couldn't truthfully say the same about Kit, who looked tired and paler than usual, as if she'd had some sleepless nights of late. On an impulse, Nell asked, 'Have you just finished work? Do you have time for a coffee?'

Kit hesitated for a moment, then burst into tears. Nell put her arms around her shoulders awkwardly, not knowing what to say. Well, knowing but not wanting to say it. Somehow, it came out anyway.

'Are you not pregnant, Kit?'

Kit didn't answer. She couldn't. She was crying too hard, and Nell couldn't tell her, Never mind. You'll have another cycle of treatment. It'll happen eventually. Because there was a strong chance that it wouldn't. Fertility treatment didn't work for everyone.

'No, Nell,' Kit finally said. 'I—Believe it or not, I am pregnant.' She made a little sound. 'That's the first time I've said it…'

'Oh, gosh, that's fabulous. That's—'

'But I'm so scared. We only just did the test yesterday. The soonest possible minute, probably.'

'That means—'

'It was one of those extra-sensitive ones that they torture fertility patients with. I almost wanted to wait, but Gian—And I understand that, and a part of me didn't want to wait either. Only it's so early, and IVF patients miscarry more often. Lots of fertile women miscarry at this point—you know that—before they'd ever have realised they were pregnant at all, only it— uh!—wouldn't be so important to them.'

'Oh, Kit…'

'And he didn't want me to work today. Which is

ridiculous, even though I felt the same, because if this isn't a viable pregnancy, lying on my side with my feet on a pillow for the next however many weeks isn't going to turn it into one, and—'

'I think you should lie down now, though. Can I get Gian to come and pick you up?'

'Oh, he's here, in surgery. Emergency Caesarean. Bonnie is with her grandmother.'

'Can I take your car and drive you home?'

'No, just sit in it with me for a while, if you can stand me venting for a bit longer.'

'Do you *feel* pregnant yet?'

'Not yet. Not at all. I want to. And I know all the symptoms, Nell! I keep smelling things to see if they'll make me queasy, and so far they don't.'

'Can I tell you that you look tired? Will that help?'

'Do I?' Kit brightened, then laughed at herself. 'Well, since I hardly slept last night… I don't think I can live through this, Nell. It's the hanging in limbo, not knowing whether to celebrate or mourn.'

'Yes, I know.' And Nell did. Too well.

'The other times,' Kit went on, 'when I was never pregnant at all, I could at least put that cycle behind me. This time…'

'Wait it out. Take it easy. That's all you can do.' She coaxed Kit in the direction of the nurses' parking area.

'And I can't tell Caroline. Not yet. I don't want to see Caroline. Not for— Not until—I hate her, Nell, just because this is easy for her!'

'Totally normal. I won't tell her.'

'I don't really hate her.'

'I know. You're allowed to feel all this, Kit. It's in the book.'

Kit laughed again 'I've read the book. All the books. Doesn't help.'

'I'm just going to sit with you in your car for a while, OK?'

'Thanks.'

After about fifteen minutes, Kit decided she was feeling rational enough to drive. 'If you end up wishing you hadn't told me,' Nell said, 'that's in the book, too.'

'I'm very lucky that you've read the book, aren't I?'

'And Gian's read it, too,' she pointed out gently. 'Be good to each other.'

When Kit had driven off, Nell crossed her fingers and prayed, remembering the way her own long-ago pregnancy had ended. If Kit lost this baby, it would be much worse.

It was time to talk to Bren.

'You can head off now, Bren, I'm sure,' said Alison Cairns, the doctor who was officially covering this shift in the emergency department.

'Well, no,' he answered, 'I can at least hang around until you've got the cardiac patient up to the ward.'

'Really, he's looking pretty stable. And IQ's just walked in, and—'

'Nell?' Bren said. 'She's back?'

'Yes, Nell. Dr Cassidy. I meant, of course.' The younger doctor blushed. 'I'm sorry, I shouldn't have— I do sometimes call her that when I'm letting off steam to my—But, really, I've learned so much from her over the past couple of years. She's amazing, actually…'

She trailed off, as if realising that her attempt to backpedal was only making her initial gaffe worse. Clearly, like Janelle Peacock a couple of weeks ago, she'd heard the rumours about Bren and Nell.

He ignored the whole thing and instead asked, 'Where is she?' That was all he really wanted to know.

'Oh, her office. Unless she's at the nurses' station by now. She'll want to catch up.'

'I bet she hasn't even been home,' Bren muttered, and went to look for her.

She was still in her office. Its door hung open to reveal an efficient working environment softened by three children's drawings depicting their hospital experiences, which Nell had had professionally framed and matted in bright colours—magenta, orange and indigo. Somehow, her choice of decoration seemed to say a lot about who she was, both the good and the less good, but these days Bren was far more interested in who she could become.

She looked up as soon as he entered the doorway.

'Oh,' she said. 'Hi.' She was wearing a pale skirt, a striped top and sandals, and she had a sheer, cinnamon-toned lipstick on her mouth, a fine gold necklace around her throat and some colour in her cheeks. She looked warm and beautiful, but—

'Tell me that's not your Brisbane suitcase sitting in the corner,' he drawled.

She frowned, tried not to look emotional about seeing him and failed. He was pleased about that. Yes, the brittle façade was definitely cracking more often now.

'Easier to have the taxi drop me off here,' she said. 'I'd only have turned around at home and got straight back in the car '

'And it's been a disaster every day you've been away,' he teased. 'Patients dying like flies, cardiac cases getting sent home with eye ointment while we do emergency surgery on the common cold. Lucky you're back to get us all shaped up again.'

She looked at him with a wooden, unreadable expression, and for a moment he bought the act and thought, No, Nell, don't do this. Tell me you knew I was trying to make you laugh. He felt his jaw tighten and his heart drop into his lower stomach.

Then she took a deep breath, cupped her newly tanned chin in her hand, kept those blue eyes shafting into his and said, 'Actually, I just wanted to see you.' Then she sighed, and smiled.

Ah, that felt good! His heart lightened like a helium balloon. He couldn't even react, wanted to say something clever or sexy or, lord, shamelessly, wantonly lovelorn. Instead, he just heard his voice drop to a husky pitch, and out came the words, 'Yeah, Nell?'

'Um, yeah. So if—if everything is as good as you tried to pretend it *wasn't*—oh, that doesn't make sense!—then, could we, if you want to, could we go somewhere—home—and talk?'

The messy speech suggested that Bren wasn't the only one having trouble here.

'You don't want to check the cardiac patient?' he asked, mostly because he was surprised that she hadn't suggested it.

How much backtracking had she done before he'd come in on who they'd had through here this past week? He'd also done a ruptured appendix and a compound leg fracture, in addition to his scheduled lists. Would she have questions on those?

And why the *hell* was he stalling her, when he wanted to do the exact opposite?

'Oh, we really do have a cardiac patient?' she said

'Stable,' he assured her quickly. 'Going to a bed upstairs. Nothing to worry about. It's been pretty quiet today. Let's go, before something happens.'

He came fully into the room, sidestepped her desk and took her hand. It felt cold, and he wondered why. She frowned at her computer, but didn't argue, so he let her go and picked up her suitcase instead.

They got to her place ten minutes later, after filling his car with some superficial stuff about her holiday and her mother, which he sensed didn't even skim the surface of what was really on her mind. She mentioned running into Kit on her way in, but didn't elaborate on that, just said she was fine.

He brought Nell's suitcase inside, not knowing whether to touch her. He wanted to, of course, but she'd said she wanted to talk, and in that area he knew they were overdue.

'So,' he said, dropping the suitcase in the hall, 'where are we talking?'

'Um…'

She didn't seem to know how to start this, so he made all the moves, leading her over to that squashy, dusky pink couch that at first glance didn't seem to fit her but, in fact, fitted her very well—fitted the woman she was becoming, not the woman she'd been.

'Sit,' he said, doing so first and then patting a place beside him, nice and close. His hand made a shallow dip for her thighs. He put his arm around her and waited, listening to the efforts and false starts she made with her breathing.

'When we split up, all those years ago,' she finally said, 'there was something else going on that I never told you about, Bren, and that I need to tell you about now, before we…well, in order for there to be, really, any chance of us going on with this. Going further.'

'Further?'

'Beyond the affair. That is—Do you want that, Bren? To go further?'

He reached out, pulled her head onto his shoulder and said, 'Way further. Don't you know that?' He could have said more, but she was the one doing the talking.

'You see, I was pregnant, Bren.'

It came out of the blue, and he didn't understand at first. 'Pregnant? You are?' The word was so strong it deafened him for a moment, and he didn't connect it to what she'd already said.

'No, I was. *Was*,' she repeated, as if he still didn't get that this was past tense, but he did get it now. 'Seventeen years ago, when we had that big fight. Only I didn't know then.'

She waited for a moment, as if he might have some response to this, but he didn't, because it was too enormous and he still had no clue where it was going. A degree of caution had kicked in, and it was possible that his body had stiffened.

'I probably should have,' she continued, speaking faster, sounding scared. 'But I didn't. When I…let myself know, let myself look at the probability of it, I just panicked. Mum realised something was up. She asked questions and got a test kit for me, so she knew for certain as soon as I did. She convinced me to have a termination.'

'Right,' Bren croaked.

'In Canberra. We drove to Canberra. I didn't want to do it. I was terrified. I kept telling myself that when we got to Canberra, got to the clinic so that it wasn't just me and Mum alone together, I'd tell her I wasn't going through with it. But I never did that.'

'So you did go through with it? You had the termination.'

'No. No, I didn't.'

'Either you did or you didn't, Nell. Where's the third option?' He knew he sounded angry.

Was he?

Should he be?

'I miscarried. That was the third option. I'd been having cramps, but I didn't realise what they were. I was so tense, I thought it was just my whole stomach balled up in a knot of apprehension. But then…' she laughed sourly '…at a petrol station on the way, in this little toilet cubicle that, let me tell you, was overdue for a clean, I just…miscarried…in a flood…and it was over, and the decision was just whipped out of my hands.'

The way she'd said it told him it hadn't felt like a relief, or a reprieve, but he still didn't understand, and didn't know how to react. He did feel angry. Was that unforgivable? Who was in the right? He couldn't speak. His head started to pound, and something acidic surged into his muscles, making them tighten and vibrate like guitar strings plucked too hard.

Finally, Nell said thinly, 'Don't you have something to say?'

'I'm trying to work out why you let nearly seventeen years go by without telling me about this.' He controlled his tone with difficulty. 'Because you didn't think it was important enough?'

She made a helpless sound, and he fought his way to his feet, needing some distance, some air, some time to think. He pressed his fingertips to his temples, and moved instinctively towards the front door.

Dear God, it would have completed his naïve, masculine, fear-motivated fantasy back then, wouldn't it? If she'd continued with the pregnancy, and he'd married her, and they'd made a struggling little family together.

She would have worked—waitressing, or something—while he'd undergone his cancer treatment and recovered from it. Then, as her stomach grew, and his fear receded, he'd have found a job himself. If they'd really pushed themselves, they might have eventually struggled through their medical degrees, possibly even their specialist training, but would they have survived the stress? Would they still be together?

He doubted it. More likely, they'd have been the absurdly young divorced parents of a sixteen-year-old, with—

'Girl or boy?' he asked suddenly.

'I never knew.'

'No, I suppose not.'

He couldn't imagine it at all, in that case, without even a gender to assign to their lost child. A sixteen-year-old, though—a rebellious boy, perhaps, or a fashion-obsessed girl. And younger siblings? A whole nest of lives. Hell, it was impossible to think of.

And she'd never told him. Not when it had happened, and not since he'd been back in Glenfallon. She was telling him now, but with such an air of built-up need and terror that he knew they hadn't got to the bottom of it yet.

Was this why she'd been holding back, insisting on the 'light' version of an involvement? He suddenly felt as if their wild, saucy love-making, their meals together, their conversations, even that visit out to her father's, had been like artificial whipped cream, with no calories, no consequences and no real satisfaction.

She should have told him sooner, if it was this important. And if she'd been this scared about how angry he'd be, then it *was* important. His circular thoughts tightened like knots, and he badly needed some air, and somewhere for his feet to go.

'I'm sorry,' he said abruptly. 'I have to go. I have to get outside. I have to think about this.'

'OK. Yes. I understand,' she said, sounding like the sixteen-year-old daughter they hadn't had.

He didn't turn and look at her, just opened the door and left, not sure when he'd come back, how he'd be feeling, or what he'd say to her when he did.

Bren had forgotten to close the door, which hung ajar about half a metre from the jamb.

It didn't matter, because the day was sunny and warm and Glenfallon didn't get a lot of home invaders showing up on a Saturday afternoon when there was a car parked in the driveway, so Nell just sat and looked at the narrow vista of the outside world that the opening afforded her.

She felt drained and completely empty. After all this time she'd finally told Bren Forsythe that the two of them might have created a child. And she'd received the reaction she'd always expected. He was angry, and he'd gone.

After a few minutes—it might have been longer, or less, but time didn't feel very relevant at the moment—Nell discovered she still wasn't sorry that the truth was out on the table. Some strength, as well as a cautious sense of validation, trickled slowly back into her empty limbs.

She hadn't needed to terminate the pregnancy in the end, and her mother had always regarded this fact as 'the best possible outcome'. Mum had said it again, just two days ago in Brisbane.

'But she's wrong,' Nell said aloud. Dad, in his way, had known that.

The miscarriage had taken away any possibility of a fight, and Nell had needed a fight. She'd needed to stand up to her mother and fight not to end the pregnancy. She'd needed to fight to bring up a child on her own, or to find the courage to have it adopted. Maybe she'd have contacted Bren if she'd had the reality of a child to consider.

Then, as the years had passed, she'd needed the firmer foundation of knowing for certain how she would have acted if the miscarriage hadn't happened. Because it was possible, too, that she'd have gone through with the termination. If she had, she would have had to learn to live with that fact.

Instead, she'd never been sure, and the doubt had

slowly poisoned her for years. She could have reconciled her own actions, whatever they might have been. Getting let off the hook had been harder in so many ways.

Now, at last, she'd told Bren, and if he wasn't planning to let her off the hook as easily as her own body once had, she was glad. She was stricken, pained, feeling as if she'd been knived in the stomach, but she was still glad.

I didn't want him to make this too easy, she realised.

She heard the sound of a vehicle coming slowly down the street and for a moment she thought, He's back! But then it finally registered that he hadn't gone off in his car in the first place. It was still parked in her drive.

Slowly, she got to her feet. Her legs felt stiff.

Was he just sitting in his front seat, or something?

She looked, but he wasn't there.

Leaving the front door open, just as he had, she went down the steps toward the front gate and out onto the concrete path that ran along in front of Grafton Street's quiet Federation houses.

OK, what next?

She looked down the street in the direction he'd have taken if he'd steamed off home on foot, but that had been…well, a while ago and, of course, he wasn't in sight. Then she looked the other way, and saw him coming towards her. She had to put her hand on the old-fashioned wooden gatepost for support.

Neither of them spoke until he was close enough to reach out and touch her. He didn't touch her, in fact, but he could have if he'd wanted to.

'Hi,' he growled at her, frowning. 'Sorry.' He had his hands in his pockets, and his shoulders were stiff. For once his short haircut looked severe and intimidating, coupled with the frown and with his dark eyes.

'I don't want you to apologise,' she said.

'I walked out on you.'

'You were angry, and you had every right to be. I should have told you. First. Instead of telling Mum. I should have chased you up in Melbourne, and—'

'Hey. Come on! No. We were kids. That's not why I'm angry. Or why I was.'

'So why are you?'

'I don't think I am now.'

'I want you to be, Bren.'

'That's perverse.'

Suddenly, she began to sob. 'No, it isn't. It's *necessary*.'

'Let's go inside.' He put his arms around her and she couldn't fight him because she was sobbing too hard. 'Tell me, Nell,' he said. 'Tell me, darling love.'

They went up the path together and into the house, and he kicked the door shut with his heel then turned her against his chest and stroked her hair, while she sobbed out everything she'd only just begun to understand about the guilt, the lack of something to fight, to fight *for* or to fight *against*, the way she'd been robbed of resolution, the anger she still felt towards her mother for seriously believing that what had happened had been 'the best outcome'.

'It felt like she was feeding me invalid custard when I needed steak bones to chew on, or something. Telling me it was all right, it was for the best, when I knew somewhere inside me that it wasn't. I'm not blaming her. Not really. But she was wrong, and I could never see why before. My whole adult life has been about apologising to our unborn baby for my ambivalence, by putting everything into my work. It doesn't make sense. I know that. But I love my work, and somehow it was easy to get onto that downward spiral of not having enough other stuff in my life.'

She stopped, and gave a helpless shrug.

'So how does it help if I'm angry?' Bren asked.

She looked up, touched his shirt where her tears had soaked it. 'Because I should have told you this weeks ago, instead of running from it.'

'You've told me now.'

'I'm lucky you're still here.' She managed to laugh through her tears, then grew serious again. 'And because I considered a termination seventeen years ago, Bren. I can't promise you that I would have stood up to my mother.'

'I can't promise you that I'd have stayed married to you, seventeen years ago, if you'd been rash enough to say yes to me. Let's forget the hypothetical scenarios.' He stroked her face, and kissed her forehead, her temple, her cheek. 'Forgive yourself, Nell, because I do, if there was anything to forgive in the first place.'

'I've started to, since you came back. That's been good. I've really worked at it. In all sorts of ways. Some of them don't make sense.'

'No?'

'I've, um, put the pizza restaurant on my speed dial, and I know you won't get why that's important, but can you celebrate about it for me anyway?'

'Woo-hoo!' he said obediently.

They both started laughing, and Nell couldn't stop.

'Hey,' Bren finally said.

'Hey, yourself.' She sniffed, didn't know if she was laughing or crying, now, and he dragged an impossibly large wad of tissues from the box on the side table and gave them to her like a bunch of flowers.

'You would have told me weeks ago, if you could have,' Bren said. 'I could see you working up to it.'

'Could you?'

'You don't always have that professional mask in place, you know.'

'I've been trying. Not to, I mean.'

'We haven't wasted much time. Just as long as we don't waste any more. I don't want an affair with you, Nell. Stop fobbing me off with that. I'm not going to take it any more. I love you.'

'And I love you, Bren, so much.' She held his face between her hands and looked into his eyes, daring to show all of it. 'I'm not fobbing you off now.'

'I want to marry you, and spend my life with you.'

'Play guitar on my veranda?'

'Please!' He kissed her. 'They want too much for that other house. Let's stay here. Let's try for a baby who's wanted and perfectly timed and ours to love and keep right from the start.'

'Could we? You want that?'

'I want everything, Nell, as long as it's with you. And I don't want to wait any longer.'

In the end, they waited for three months, and had a January wedding.

They could have managed it sooner, but they both discovered a streak of unabashed romanticism in their attitude that made it imperative to get the timing and the occasion itself just right. No rushing through the details, no regrets later about inadequate photos and insufficient food.

Nell wanted to wait until Kit's pregnancy was well established, publicly announced and showing the right healthy signs, which by January it was. Nell and Bren had decided to try for a baby straight away, as soon as they were married, and she was very happy to give Kit at least a four-month head start.

At the sunset wedding, held in the back garden of her own house, Kit's pregnancy had just begun to show, while Caroline was now looking enormous and was grateful for the late afternoon breeze, dry air and plentiful supplies of juice and mineral water.

'You should have issued a separate invitation for the baby,' Caroline joked, as they sipped champagne and ate canapés after the ceremony.

Her husband Declan stood at her side, and added, 'If she was any bigger, Nell, you couldn't have fitted in all your guests. The garden looks beautiful.'

'We got professionals in,' Bren told him. 'Didn't want weeds and brown flower-heads showing in the photos.'

Actually, that had been Nell's mother's idea. Mum was here, of course, chatting with Dad about his honey at the moment. They looked nicely at ease with each other.

'I did spot a couple of dead-heads,' Emma said. She was a keen gardener. 'But I won't tell you where they are! Not in the photos, I'm sure.' She grinned.

Emma and Pete hadn't said anything about their own plans, but Nell suspected they were trying for a baby now, too. Pete's girls would adore a baby brother or sister, now that they'd settled into Pete and Emma's new marriage.

Remembering all the 'Single Professional Women's Club' activities they'd engaged in over the past couple of years—the wine-tasting tour, the self-taught massage course, the video marathon and Emma's gourmet cooking classes imported from Paris—Nell wondered what the four women would all be doing together this time next year, or the year after that.

Play-groups and picnics? Babysitting exchanges and group visits to story time at the local library? Wouldn't it be good? So far from what she'd imagined less than six months ago, and so much better.

'What are you thinking?' Bren came up to her from behind, and rested his chin on her shoulder so he could nuzzle her ear as he whispered into it.

'I'm not thinking, I'm marvelling,' Nell said.

'So am I.' He kissed her neck, and wrapped his arms around her waist. The silk fabric whispered against her skin, and she closed her hands over his. 'Can we remember how marvelling feels, do you think, and keep marvelling about this forever?'

'Oh, yes! Yes, please!'

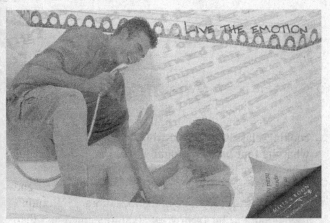

MILLS & BOON®

Live the emotion

_MedicaL
romance™

BUSHFIRE BRIDE by *Marion Lennox*

Dr Rachel Harper just wanted to escape her busy emergency ward for a weekend. Now she's stranded in the Outback, working with the area's only doctor, the powerfully charming Hugo McInnes. Soon their attraction is raging as strongly as the bushfires around town – but Rachel's secret means she can't give in to her awakened feelings…

THE DOCTOR'S SECRET FAMILY by *Alison Roberts*

It was love at first sight for Dr Hannah Campbell and surgeon Jack Douglas. But all too soon Hannah learned that Jack had been keeping a crucial secret from her. Now Jack is working on her paediatric ward, and she wants nothing to do with him. She can't risk him seeing her daughter…*his* daughter!

THE PREGNANT MIDWIFE by *Fiona McArthur*

(Marriage and Maternity)

Midwife Kirsten Wilson has been trying to forget Hunter Morgan since returning to Sydney. Getting up in the helicopter again, to rescue tiny babies, is just what she needs. At least until Hunter arrives as the new doctor in charge! Then a huge helicopter crash forces them to put their priorities in order – and changes their lives for ever…

On sale 6th August 2004

Available at most branches of WHSmith, Tesco, Martins, Borders, Eason, Sainsbury's and all good paperback bookshops.

MILLS & BOON®

Live the emotion

_MedicaL
romance™

EMERGENCY: BACHELOR DOCTOR
by Gill Sanderson *(Special Care Baby Unit)*

On her first day at the Wolds Hospital, Dr Kim Hunter
was not expecting to work in the Special Care Baby
Unit – and neither was she expecting the impact that
her new colleague, Dr Harry Black, had on her! Kim
found herself falling for him, and then discovered the
heartbreaking reasons behind his fear of commitment…

RAPID RESPONSE *by Jennifer Taylor*

(A&E Drama)

Two years ago Holly Daniels's fiancé walked out
without warning – and now the two specialist registrars
are reunited, forced to work side by side in the Rapid
Response team of a busy emergency unit. Holly's
surprised at how fast her heart reacts to Ben Carlisle,
and Ben is just as quick to react – so why did he walk
away in the first place…?

DOCTORS IN PARADISE *by Meredith Webber*

Tranquillity Sands is a health resort set on a coral-
fringed island surrounded by the Pacific – what could
possibly go wrong in this perfect place? Everything, as
far as Dr Caroline Sayers is concerned! She finds
herself in the midst of intrigue, superstition and medical
emergency – and through it all strolls Dr Lucas Quinn:
laid-back, caring…and utterly irresistible!

On sale 6th August 2004

*Available at most branches of WHSmith, Tesco, Martins, Borders,
Eason, Sainsbury's and all good paperback bookshops.*

MILLS & BOON

Volume 2
on sale from
6th August
2004

Lynne
Graham
International Playboys

A Savage
Betrayal

4 FREE
books and a surprise gift!

We would like to take this opportunity to thank you for reading this Mills & Boon® book by offering you the chance to take FOUR more specially selected titles from the Medical Romance™ series absolutely FREE! We're also making this offer to introduce you to the benefits of the Reader Service™—

> ★ FREE home delivery
> ★ FREE gifts and competitions
> ★ FREE monthly Newsletter
> ★ Exclusive Reader Service offers
> ★ Books available before they're in the shops

Accepting these FREE books and gift places you under no obligation to buy, you may cancel at any time, even after receiving your free shipment. Simply complete your details below and return the entire page to the address below. *You don't even need a stamp!*

YES! Please send me 4 free Medical Romance books and a surprise gift. I understand that unless you hear from me, I will receive 6 superb new titles every month for just £2.69 each, postage and packing free. I am under no obligation to purchase any books and may cancel my subscription at any time. The free books and gift will be mine to keep in any case.

M4ZED

Ms/Mrs/Miss/Mr ....Initials................................
                                                                    BLOCK CAPITALS PLEASE
Surname ....
Address ....
....
....Postcode..............................

Send this whole page to:
UK: FREEPOST CN81, Croydon, CR9 3WZ
EIRE: PO Box 4546, Kilcock, County Kildare (stamp required)